Norma

SLEEPING DOGS II

By

Norma E. Rawlings

Castle of Dreams Books

First impression

Published by

Castle of Dreams Books
8 Pease Street
Darlington
DL1 4EU
UK

dreamer@dial.pipex.com

☏ 01325 381466

This is a work of fiction, any resemblance to persons, living, or dead, is purely coincidental.

By the same author: ***Sleeping Dogs***

ISBN 1 86185 231 2

ACKNOWLEDGEMENTS

Mr Dirk Fitz-Hugh of the Anglo-German Family History Society, for the Berlin photographs and documents.

The Oxford Central Library

Nando, for his information on Portugal

My doctor, for her medical advice

DEDICATION

To my twin granddaughters
Amelia May and Jade Elizabeth

LIST OF CHARACTERS

Thomas Kendal	An Oxford student
Joanna Kendal	Thomas's mother
Emma Westlake	Thomas's maternal grandmother
Marcus Westlake	Thomas's maternal grandfather
Burrows and Stephens	The Westlake's Chauffeurs
John Peterson	Thomas's bodyguard (as a child)
Ben	The Westlake's gardener
Tim	Ben's son
Gus and Kal	Thomas's friends at Oxford
Felicity Shaw (Fliss)	An Oxford student
Andrew Shaw	Felicity's grandfather, retired head of Special Branch
Sally Bennett	An Oxford student
Richard and Molly Bennett	Sally's parents
Henry Kendal	Thomas's paternal grandfather
Penny Kendal	Thomas's paternal grandmother
Amy Brent	Thomas's aunt
Joel Brent	Amy's husband
Judy and Jo	Sally's flatmates
Jack and Mary Oliver	Amy's staff
Mr Abercrombie	A private detective

SOMETHING TO THINK ABOUT...

We are as we think we are
But that is just not so,
If we trace our families back
As far as we can go,
We will most surely find
People of a different kind,
Passing their genes down the line
Every part of us, you know
Is theirs from head to toe.
We are as we think we are
But that is just not so...

CHAPTERS

PROLOGUE

1ST NOVEMBER 1991

It was morning. The fields, lakes and trees in the Lake district were covered in a fine soft mist – grey and silent.

Westlake Manor, which stood near the cold, still waters of Lake Windermere, was a hive of activity. Lord and Lady Westlake, Marcus and Emma, lived there with their widowed daughter, Joanna Kendal, whose husband had been murdered in London, in the March of that year. He had died not knowing he was going to be a father.

Joanna's baby was due. Her contractions had started early that morning, and were getting stronger and more frequent. Emma Westlake was helping her daughter collect the bag for her confinement, whilst Marcus rang the private nursing home to tell them that Joanna was on her way, and telling the chauffeur, Stephens, to bring the car round to the front door.

Marcus and Emma helped their daughter out to the car. Stephens threw his cigarette end out of the car window, and hastily got out to open the doors and put Joanna's bag into the boot.

Marcus got into the front of the car, whilst Joanna and her mother sat in the back. They set off. Stephens driving carefully along the winding, misty roads. Joanna leaned her head back against the seat of the car. Her blue eyes closed, her lovely face set in fleeting anguish. One slender hand went up to stroke her long golden hair, which was tied back in a navy chiffon bow. Her hand moved down over her loose navy dress and rested on her swollen body. Her other hand clutched her mother's – a hand that was growing old gracefully with brown speckles on her fair skin, and slightly raised veins. Both women had beautifully manicured fingernails, and both wore expensive diamond rings.

They soon arrived at the nursing home. Stephens, a big middle–aged man with neat greying hair, got swiftly out of the car and opened the doors. They all got out and headed for the main door, Stephens following with the bag. They were greeted by a nurse who took Joanna's bag.

"You can go now, Stephens," said Marcus quietly, "We will ring you when we want picking up."

"Right–o, Sir," replied Stephens, who ambled back to the smart black Rolls–Royce.

They were taken to the reception desk where Joanna had to check in. A nurse then took her upstairs in a smooth quiet lift, for her to be examined by the doctor and put to bed.

"You may see your daughter shortly," smiled the smart receptionist. "If you would like to go along to the waiting room, someone will bring you some coffee."

"Thank you," replied Emma, returning her smile. The Westlakes walked into the empty waiting room opposite, and took off their coats, and put them onto a chair, along with Emma's soft black leather Gucci handbag. They walked over to the window and looked forlornly out onto the garden, where shrubs and trees peeped out of the rising mist.

"I hope she's going to be alright," said Emma anxiously, stroking her soft golden hair behind her ears, which were small and neat, each boasting a sparkling diamond.

"She's young and strong – of course she will be alright," replied her husband kindly.

They stood silent for a moment – a tall, handsome, couple in their late forties. Marcus looked down at his wife, fondly with warm grey eyes, which blended so well with his thick silver hair and small silver moustache that grew neatly over thin, firm lips.

"It's such a shame about Thomas. Joanna misses him so much," murmured Emma.

"They never did catch the blighter who shot him," returned Marcus, "it's a disgrace!"

Emma looked uncomfortable. She brushed an imaginary speck off her white mohair sweater and long dark grey skirt. "I still don't agree with her not telling Thomas's parents about the baby. They have a right to know," she whispered guiltily.

"I know, but it's her wish," he replied. The door suddenly opened, and a nurse came in with a tray of coffee, followed by two more people who went and sat down in a couple of armchairs. The nurse put down the tray of coffee by a settee, and Marcus and Emma sat down. Emma poured their coffee. Marcus looked up at the "no-smoking" sign on the wall. "Look at that damned thing!" he scowled, patting the breast pocket of his tweed jacket, where a packet of cigars was hiding. The couple opposite smiled.

A little while later the Westlakes were allowed to see their daughter. She was lying propped up in bed in her private room. Her blue eyes lit up at the sight of her parents.

"They've given me an epidural," she smiled, "I won't have any pain."

The Westlakes stayed with their daughter. Four hours later she gave birth to a son.

He was named Thomas Kendal junior.

CHAPTER ONE

THOMAS GOES TO OXFORD – 2010

Thomas Kendal was brought up in a life of wealth and luxury. He had been born a beautiful child with curly golden hair and sapphire eyes like his father. He had a sunny disposition and was loved by everyone – his mother, Marcus and Emma, his nanny, the chauffeur, the gardener, cook and housekeeper, and everyone who came into contact with him.

As he grew older he was given the best of everything, and even had his own pony by the time he was five years old. He grew up a warm, friendly, unspoilt and loving child. His mother sent him to the best private schools in the district. Burrows, the new family chauffeur, and a bodyguard, John Peterson, took him to school. Thomas was not allowed to 'board' at school, his mother wanted to keep him at home, as she felt he would be safer. Westlake Manor was fully alarmed. The Westlakes were terrified in case he was kidnapped.

Thomas was an intelligent boy, and soon began to notice his mother's strange attitude. She hated people who were not perfect or of the 'upper class'. She chose all Thomas's friends and would not let him have anything to do with people who were black, or disabled, which left him puzzled, as he liked everybody. If he ever questioned her she would always get him to back down. Thomas thought his mother was so beautiful, and when she put on her 'sad face' he would always give in to her.

The Westlakes had a gardener called Ben Harrison, a quiet, middle-aged man, who had a son called Tim. Tim was the same age as Thomas, but backward. He was thin with dark hair and sad brown eyes. Thomas liked Tim, and the two lads loved to play football together and chase each other through the trees. Ben would often take the two boys fishing during the school holidays, and they would sit on the bank and enjoy a picnic, which Ben's wife had provided with loving care. Thomas loved it.

When Joanna found out she had been furious. She had shouted at Thomas and made him cry, and yelled and screamed at John Peterson for allowing the friendship. John Peterson was a retired soldier – big and strong with legs like tree trunks. He had short, grey hair and steely eyes. He was not the slightest bit afraid of Joanna, and would simply stick a finger up at her behind her back, and continue to let Thomas play with Tim. Thomas thought he was wonderful!

By the time he was seventeen he had grown into a very clever and handsome young man. He had grown tall, his shoulders broad, and he looked like his father with a straight nose, slightly full lips and even white teeth, but his eyes, although sapphire like his father's, were warm and smiling. His father's had been hard and watchful.

Young Thomas was very proud of his dead father, and loved to hear all the wonderful things that people said about him. His mother had adored him and always kept a large photo of him and herself on their wedding day, which was kept in the drawing room.

Thomas Kendal senior had been an up-and-coming M.P. He and Joanna had lived in London. Thomas snr. had been a very popular M.P. He had been a wonderful speaker and would mesmerise crowds with his rich, warm voice. He had also been very generous and had often given money to good causes, such as donating funds to the opening of homes and shelters for third world refugees, crippled children and down-and-outs. He had even been given the nick–name of St. Thomas, and was destined, according to the press, to be a future Prime Minister.

In the March of 1991 Thomas snr. had gone to Walthamstow, to the opening of a clinic, Kendrick House, to help drug addicts. At the opening was a pop singer called Nico Tolly. Nico had received a couple of death threats the week before, but had ignored them. During the opening Thomas snr. had been shot and killed. The police had said that the target had been Nico Tolly, and Thomas had been shot by mistake. It had been a terrible tragedy. The killer never found.

Young Thomas wanted to be like his father and become an M.P. He wanted to do all the good things his father had done. His mother was thrilled and gave him every encouragement.

The only thing that now puzzled Thomas was his mother's attitude to minority groups. If she had hated them so much, why did she support his father's actions, and how had he put up with her?

Thomas was finding his mother more difficult, the older he got. She insisted on picking his friends and girl friends, and had already selected him a wife.

"For God's sake, Mother, I can pick my own friends!" he would say to her.

"But, Thomas, darling," she would cry, "I only want the best for you."

By the time Thomas was almost 19 he was ready to go to Oxford University. He had got a place at Keble, and was going to study law. Thomas was happy and excited. He often felt like a prisoner living at Westlake Manor, and couldn't wait to get away and have some freedom. He had told his mother he did not want a bodyguard at Oxford, and, thankfully, he was supported by his grandfather who had sided with him.

"Don't be silly, Joanna, he is old enough to stand on his own two feet, don't mollycoddle him." John Peterson left the household, still on good terms with Thomas.

The day finally arrived for Thomas to go to Oxford. Due to the restrictions on cars in many big cities, particularly Oxford, Thomas had been forced to leave his precious car at home, and would be taken down to Oxford by Burrows.

The car eventually rolled smoothly out of the drive, his mother and grandparents waving frantically from the house.

Thomas leaned his fair head against the back of the seat, smacked the palms of his hands down onto his thighs, and let out a long sigh. Freedom at last! Thomas was cheerful, happy, and carefree.

He had no idea of the horrors that were waiting for him in the wings of his life.

Thomas loved Oxford. It was a place so full of life and people. The buildings were mixtures of old and new – ancient buildings set amongst supermarkets and fast food shops, and there was so much to do. There were so many pubs and bars and nightclubs and restaurants for every kind of food. There were theatres and cinemas and museums and endless places of interest. Thomas was lucky that he could afford a smart rented flat, situated between the railway station and the canal. It was only a short walk from Keble, a lovely, old red brick building. The flat gave him a great sense of freedom, as many students had to share with others to cover the cost of rent.

Thomas had a wonderful time at Oxford. He got on well with everyone, students and lecturers. He had never known so many beautiful, intelligent girls, who all adored him. Thomas was able to do all the things he had not been able to do at home, such as pub-crawling, night–clubbing, going for Chinese and Indian meals, and eating pizzas and beefburgers, and fish and chips straight out of the paper bag whilst walking along the streets. He could stagger about drunk and silly with his pals, talk gibberish and giggle, and wake up with hang–overs saying 'never again'. Thomas had many girlfriends, some of them staying the night at his flat, and sometimes they would even clean up the flat for him, as he had not got a clue about housework and cooking. His independence now denied him a cleaning lady!

Thomas made two good friends at Oxford and they ended up going everywhere together. They were Gus and Kal. Kal was studying law with Thomas. He was a half–caste, his father Portuguese and his mother Indian. Kal was tall, dark and handsome with his shining, short black hair, his teeth even and white. He came from a rich family and was very polite and reserved. Gus was the total opposite to Thomas and Kal. He was tall and thin with very long legs. His long light brown hair was tied back in a ponytail, and large rimless glasses, which hid a pair of intelligent grey eyes, rested on his bony nose. Gus's father was a history professor who had passed on his passion of the ancient world to his son. Gus was full of confidence and more worldly-wise than Thomas and Kal, who had both led rather sheltered lives. Gus shared a flat with Kal and looked after his rather timid flatmate. The three lads got on well, Gus and Thomas teasing Kal mercilessly when he occasionally struggled with the English language.

Everyone at Keble knew who Thomas was. People would nudge each other and say, "that's Thomas Kendal, the son of the M.P. who got shot." Thomas was soon a celebrity, but he took it all in his stride. He was quick to learn and sailed through his exams.

The weeks and months flew by. Thomas hated going home during the breaks. Although his grandparents were always thrilled to see him, his mother was horrified to see his now smooth hair growing long, and starting to curl at the ends, and his designer clothes being put aside for jeans and T-shirts with logos on the front and back.

There were many students at Keble from all walks of life. One of them was a tall, graceful girl, with long red hair, which set off her green eyes and freckled face. She was the granddaughter of Andrew Shaw, who had been the Head of Special Branch when Thomas's father had been killed. Her name was Felicity, known to her friends as Fliss.

She was the first person to ripple the smooth waters of Thomas's happy life.

CHAPTER TWO

A PUZZLE FOR THOMAS – 2011

Felicity Shaw was older than Thomas, and was in her last year at university. Her father owned a travel agency, and she had been studying languages, as she wanted to be a tour guide and travel the world. During the holidays she worked at the travel agency and was getting to know the ropes well.

During the Easter holidays of 2011 she had worked at the travel agency as usual – she had one term left at university, and in the summer she would be working full time for her father.

On the Sunday before she was due back at Oxford, Felicity had arranged to go over and visit her grandparents, who lived in a lovely old house on the outskirts of Borehamwood. Her grandfather had worked in London all his life and was now happily retired.

She drove the short distance to their home, parked her car on the drive and let her self in the back door. She waltzed through the kitchen and into the living room where her grandparents were sitting drinking a cup of tea and chatting. Rusty the dog immediately got up and started to bark and wag his tail at the sight of her.

"Fliss, my dear," cried her grandmother with a big smile, which lit up her wrinkled face.

"Hi, Gran, how are you?" she grinned. Her grandfather stood up, came over to her, and gave her a big hug.

"It's good to see you, lassie – you are staying for dinner?" he asked anxiously. She nodded and his green eyes lit up. He adored his granddaughter – she was the only grandchild who had inherited his colouring and his personality.

"Yes, I am, Gramps" she grinned back. Her grandmother fussed over her, and fetching another cup poured her a cup of tea. She sat on the settee beside her grandfather, the dog sitting by her feet, gently beating his tail against her legs.

Fliss was fond of her grandparents, and knew she didn't visit them often enough, and they were getting old. They were both well in their seventies now. Andrew was a tall, well–built man, who had been in the army in his early years. His red hair was now thin and grey making his face look round and chubby. Her grandmother, June, seemed to have shrunk over the years and was now small and thin, but she was still pretty with her brown eyes twinkling under a cap of snowy white hair, which curled round her ears. She was still sprightly and was soon bobbing about the kitchen cooking a delicious Sunday dinner.

After dinner Fliss helped her grandmother fill up the dishwasher and tidy the kitchen, then the two women went into the living room to join Andrew Shaw. Whilst they were chatting the warmth of the room sent her grandmother to sleep in the armchair, and the dog,an elderly cocker spaniel, to sleep on the floor. He lay there on his back, his paws hanging in the air.

"Well, Fliss, you've nearly finished at Oxford, have you enjoyed it?"

"Oh, yes, I've loved it!" she replied happily. They continued talking when Fliss suddenly remembered Thomas. "Gramps," she said excitedly, "you'll never guess who I've seen at Keble! He's in his first year, he's younger than me."

"Who's that?" he replied chuckling.

"Thomas Kendal," she replied. Her grandfather's silence was absolute. He eventually replied, with a frown.

"Thomas Kendal?"

"Yes," she continued. "You know, the son of Thomas Kendal, the M.P. who got shot all those years ago."

The colour drained out of Andrew Shaw's face.

"Thomas Kendal, the M.P. didn't have any children," he replied slowly, trying to keep the tremor out of his voice.

"Well," she replied gaily," he did – his mother must have been pregnant when his father was killed."

Andrew Shaw's face turned grey, and his eyes filled with fear.

"Are you all right, Gramps?" asked Fliss, puzzled. Her grandfather looked hard at her.

"What is he like?" he snapped.

Fliss was confused at her grandfather's sudden change of mood.

"He's about 20...tall...blond...blue eyes...he comes from the Lake District..." she broke off, feeling uneasy.

Andrew Shaw got up from the settee and walked over to the window, running his big fingers through what was left of his hair. "Christ Almighty," he cursed under his breath.

"Gramps, what's wrong... what's the matter?" she begged, her green eyes wide and anxious.

"Let me think!" he replied distractedly.

Fliss sat and stared at her grandfather as he started pacing the room, mumbling to himself. She looked down at her hands and started twining her fingers nervously.

"Excuse me a minute, Fliss, I'm going to my study," he suddenly stated, and marched out into the hall, went across to his study, and shut the door firmly.

Fliss looked across at her sleeping grandmother, crept out of the room, and moved silently to the study door. She heard her grandfather's voice.

"Andrew here...OK thanks...I've got bad news...remember Thomas Kendal?..the bastard had a son...of course I'm sure...Fliss told me...he's at Oxford...no I haven't...I don't know...Joanna must have been pregnant at his funeral, she kept bloody quiet...it didn't occur to me either...he'll have to be watched...I'll ask her...I'll be in touch."

Fliss slipped into the downstairs bathroom and sat on the toilet, her long fingers rubbing her cold cheeks. What was wrong with Gramps? Why was he so worried that Thomas Kendal had had a son? What had he done?

"Fliss, where are you?" called Andrew, alarmed.

"I'm in the loo, Gramps," she called out. She stood up and flushed the toilet, ran water into the basin and finally emerged.

"Gramps," she looked at him sternly, "What is going on?"

Andrew stood firmly facing her, his big hands on her shoulders–green eyes looking hard into green eyes.

"Fliss," he said slowly, "I can't tell you, but I want you to do something for me." She nodded silently. "I want you to check up on young Thomas for me. I want to know whether he is...good or bad...kind or unkind...what his beliefs are...anything, and report back to me – and don't tell anyone."

"OK," she replied uncertainly.

At that moment her grandmother came into the hall, Rusty, her shadow, trotting along behind her. "What are you two up to?"

"Nothing, dear, how about making us all a nice cup of tea?"

"Oh, yes," answered his wife," and I've got some nice fruit cake."

Fliss stayed for some tea with her grandparents, and then drove home. Her mind was in a whirl – what bombshell had she just dropped on her poor grandfather?

Fliss returned to Oxford the following morning. She, too, like Thomas, hated leaving her car at home, but her father drove her there, and would pick her up when she came home. Fliss was silent during the journey. She was wondering how she was going to meet up with Thomas Kendal. She only had one term left, and Thomas was in a different year and they both went to different lectures. Thomas, being so good-looking, was always surrounded by girls. Her task was going to be difficult.

"You're quiet, Fliss," remarked her father.

"Sorry, Dad, I was daydreaming," she replied sweetly.

Fliss was getting anxious. She had now been back at Oxford for two weeks and she still had not managed to get close enough to Thomas Kendal to even speak to him, although she had been listening to other people talking about him, and had managed to butt in with a few questions. She decided to ring her grandfather.

"Hi, Gramps, it's me, Fliss," she said gaily to him on the phone.

"Ah, Fliss, my wee lassie, what have you got for me?"

"It's not been easy, Gramps, our paths never cross, but I have got some snippets for you."

"Good girl," he replied cheerfully, "fire away!"

"Well, he's very popular and charming and very nice. He seems to be a kind–hearted person."

"What sort of people does he like and dislike?" urged Andrew Shaw.

"Well," she replied, taken aback by the question, "he likes everybody. His two best pals are as different as chalk and cheese."

"Tell me about them," Andrew Shaw butted in. Fliss frowned for a moment.

"Gus is a tall, thin guy with glasses and a ponytail, he's quite studious, but has a great sense of humour. Then there is Kal, he's a coloured lad. He comes from Portugal. He's quite posh in a foreign sort of way."

"A coloured lad, you say?" interrupted her grandfather.

"Yes," she replied, puzzled.

"Well, well," murmured Andrew Shaw. "Anything else?"

"Not really," was the slow reply.

"Keep up the good work, Fliss."

"I will, bye for now, Gramps." Andrew Shaw could hear the smile in her voice.

Fliss still struggled to get close to Thomas Kendal. Sometimes she didn't even set eyes on him for days. But one day, Fate held out a helping hand.

One warm summer's evening, Fliss and one of her classmates, Julie, a small, dainty fair–haired girl, had been to the Apollo Theatre in George Street to see a musical. As they came out they spotted the "Wig and Pen" pub opposite.

"Let's go in there for a drink, Fliss," suggested Julie. The pub was quite large and trendy with a wooden floor and spindly tables and chairs. As they walked into the half-full pub the two girls spotted Thomas, Gus and Kal sitting near the window.

"Look," whispered Julie, "there's Kal D'Sara – I think he's gorgeous– he's like Omar Sharif when he was young." Although the star had been retired many years Julie had seen him in many old films. Without warning Julie marched up to the trio and shouted. "Look, the three Musketeers!" Gus looked up to see a petite blonde and a tall redhead standing by their table.

"Hey fellas," exclaimed Gus, "Two birds!" He grinned at them both. "Come and join us."

"You can't have them both!" piped up Thomas. They all laughed and Julie sat down between Kal and Thomas, and Fliss sat down between Thomas and Gus.

"What would you like, girls?" asked Gus, unfolding his long body from the chair.

"Half a lager, please, and we'll buy the next round," replied Fliss smiling. Gus went over to the bar and got the girls a drink. Fliss turned to look at Thomas, to find him gazing at her with teasing eyes. Her heart flipped over.

"I'm Thomas Kendal, and what is your name – my goddess with the red hair..?" Fliss found herself blushing. "I'm Felicity Shaw – pleased to meet you, Thomas."

"Ignore him, Felicity," grinned Gus, pushing his glasses along his bony nose with slender fingers. "Women are not safe with our Tom!" They all laughed.

"All my friends call me Fliss," she continued. Thomas touched her glorious hair. "I shall call you Ginger," he stated calmly.

"It's not ginger," she retorted, pretending to be cross.

The five of them sat chatting and drinking and making friends, and telling each other about their careers and futures. At one stage Fliss asked Thomas, "Aren't you the son of Thomas Kendal, the M.P. who got shot?"

"Yes, I am," he replied.

"You must be very proud of him," she stated

Thomas was pleased.

"Yes, I am – I want to be just like him. I'm going into politics as soon as I finish here."

"Good for you!" she replied smiling.

Fliss and Thomas continued to chat and got on well together, but much to her disappointment a crowd of students came bowling through the pub door and surrounded them. There was much laughter and chatter and noise! Her conversation with Thomas was lost.

By eleven o'clock they all left the pub and drifted off to their own accommodation, until Fliss and Julie were once again on their own. "That Kal is a dream," murmured Julie.

"Hard luck, Ju," replied Fliss, "we'll be gone from here in 3 weeks and you'll never see him again."

"I know. Life's a bitch!"

"Have you heard from London about that interpreter's job yet?" she asked Julie.

"Yes, I've got an interview in four weeks time."

"That's great," answered Fliss, genuinely pleased for her friend.

"You're lucky," added Julie, "you've got a ready-made job with your father. When do you start?"

"As soon as I get home. I can't wait." was the reply.

The two girls parted company and went to their own rooms.

During the next couple of weeks Fliss would often see Thomas. He would shout to her, "Hi, there, Ginger!" and she would shake a friendly fist at him.

The week before the end of term they were all taking exams. Fliss bumped into Thomas one evening after a stressful day, and they went off for a pizza and a drink together. They talked for hours, about their hopes and dreams and about their childhoods. When Thomas told Fliss that by the time he was seventeen his mother had already picked him a bride, she roared with laughter.

The two of them got on so well they met every evening. Fliss liked Thomas very much, he really was the nicest man she had ever met, and insisted that they go to the summer ball together on their last night. Thomas readily agreed.

Before the ball, Fliss rang her grandfather to give her report.

"Hi, Gramps, it's me."

"Ah, Fliss, what have you got to tell me?"

"Nothing drastic, Gramps. He's like I told you before, he's kind, friendly and cheerful. He's no particular dislikes or hang-ups. If a person walked into a room with two heads Thomas would be the first person to go over to them and make them welcome."

"He seems OK then," replied Andrew Shaw.

When Fliss rang off, her grandfather shook his head. "Let's just hope he never has any children," he thought to himself as he picked up the phone.

When Thomas met Fliss at the ball she took his breath away. She looked so lovely – tall and graceful and wearing a slinky emerald dress which matched her lovely green eyes, and stopped just above the knees of her long, shapely legs. They had an unforgettable evening of eating, drinking, dancing and laughing and fooling about.

Towards the end of the evening they were both a little drunk, kissing and giggling. They were dancing slowly, holding each other close, and Thomas was trying to kiss her nose, saying he was trying to kiss each freckle.

"Thomas Kendal, you are an idiot!" she laughed in his ear.

"An idiot!" he exclaimed, "that's not a nice thing to say when I've bought you a present."

"A prezzie," she giggled, "where is it?"

"In my room," he replied, nuzzling her neck.

"I've heard that one before, Thomas," she laughed.

"It's true, it's true, I have got you a prezzie–cross my heart and hope to die!"

Thomas took hold of her hand and dragged her out of the building and along the warm, quiet, balmy streets to his flat. They both stumbled up the steps to his door, where Thomas fumbled for his key and eventually managed to unlock the door. He took her into his bedroom and sat her on the bed. She watched whilst he opened a drawer and brought out a small exquisitely wrapped box. He sat down beside her on the bed and smiled. "For you, Ginger." He gave her the gift.

Fliss sat and carefully opened the box, and pulled out something wrapped in thick tissue paper. She unwrapped the paper and gasped, "Oh, Thomas!" The gift was a small ginger cat made in delicate pottery. It looked so real. She stroked it gently with a trembling finger, as tears of joy trickled down her face. Thomas lifted her chin with his finger.

"I saw it and thought of you," he whispered, and stroked the tears from her cheeks with gentle fingers, and began kissing her face and neck. Fliss was filled with an emotion such as she had never known. She wound her arms round Thomas's neck and whispered.

"I don't care if your father was a naughty boy, you are divine...Oh, Thomas..." She kissed him passionately.

The little ginger cat slid gently onto the thick carpet.

Thomas was woken the next morning by the sun streaming through his bedroom window. He turned and smiled at the sight of Fliss's flaming red hair cascading over his pillow. He turned and slid an arm round her naked body and kissed the back of her head. She turned round to face him and looked at him with sleepy eyes.

"Good morning, Ginger," his eyes smiled at her.

"Thomas Kendal, you are a naughty boy, " she said softly. "You bought me a present, and then seduced me!" She prodded his smooth chest with a slender finger. Something stirred in Thomas's brain. He frowned.

"What was that you were saying last night about my father being a naughty boy?" Fliss froze. She bit her lip and turned her head away.

"God," she thought, "what have I done?"

"Come on, Fliss," he urged gently, "what did you mean?" She lay still and silent. Thomas cupped her chin and turned her face towards him. "Don't leave me in suspense, tell me," he begged.

Fliss took a deep breath. "I don't know much," she replied quietly.

"Just tell me," he pleaded.

She looked into his handsome, anxious face. "I think he was being watched by Special Branch."

"What!" exclaimed Thomas, "why?"

"I don't know why," she answered sadly. Thomas stroked the hair back from her face.

"Well, what makes you think that, Fliss?"

She looked at him, her eyes now wide-awake. "A few months ago I was talking to my grandfather – the one who was head of Special Branch when your father was an M.P. I just happened to mention that you were at Oxford, and he was horrified. The idea that your father had had a son upset him dreadfully. He went off to phone someone."

"Who did he phone?" asked Thomas, puzzled.

"I don't know," she replied, "but it must have been someone who knew me, because I heard him say, "Fliss told me, he's at Oxford." I can only think it was one of his old friends from work. It could have been Uncle David or his assistant Peter something..."

"Who's Uncle David?"

"He's David Clayton. He was Detective Chief Superintendent at Scotland Yard. They've been lifelong friends, they were in the army together."

"Bloody hell!" exclaimed Thomas, "what on earth could my father have done?"

"I've no idea, Thomas, I've thought and thought, but I just haven't a clue. Gramps was more concerned about your existence than anything else." Thomas felt at a loss.

"But I never knew my father," he went on. "Whatever he may have done can't possibly affect me."

"I know," she replied, "I can't understand it at all." Thomas looked at her sad face.

"I'm sorry, Thomas," she whispered.

"Don't worry, Fliss." She looked at her watch.

"Thomas, I'll have to go. It's nine-thirty and my dad's coming to pick me up at eleven, and I have to pack and say 'goodbye' to everyone." She slid out of bed and scooped up her clothes from the floor. "Where's the bathroom?"

"First door on the right. I'll make us some coffee."

"Thanks, Thomas. Milk, no sugar." She dashed off to the bathroom.

Thomas lay staring at the ceiling. He was frowning – his face serious. He was totally bewildered by what Fliss had told him. He got up when he heard the shower running, pulled on his boxer shorts and a short, thin dressing gown, and wandered into the kitchen. He rinsed his hands and face at the kitchen sink and set about making the coffee.

Fliss showered and dressed, went into the bedroom to collect her small handbag and the ginger cat, and made her way to the kitchen. She sat at the table with Thomas and they drank their coffee.

"Thomas, thank you so much for my ginger cat, I shall treasure it always." She smiled at him. Thomas looked serious.

"Don't leave me, Fliss."

"I have to go, Thomas."

"Stay here and marry me," he suggested. Fliss laughed.

"Don't be silly, Thomas. I'm ready to go to work for my father, remember. I'm, going to travel all over the world. And anyway, your mother wouldn't approve of me – and you know that's true."

Thomas leaned back in his chair.

"Too true! But I will miss you."

"I'll miss you, too." She hesitated for a moment. "Thomas, if I ever find out anything about your father, I'll let you know, and that's a promise."

"Thanks, Fliss, I would be grateful." She got up to go.

"I shall call my cat KAT," she stated, "like your initials backwards."

Thomas got up and slowly walked with her to the door. They looked at each other sadly, and kissed.

"Goodbye, Fliss."

"Goodbye, Thomas."

He stood and watched her walk down the stairs until she disappeared from sight.

Felicity Shaw just walked out of Thomas's life.

CHAPTER THREE

THOMAS STARTS A SEARCH – SUMMER 2011

After leaving Thomas's flat Fliss walked hastily back to her own room. Hot tears trickled down her freckled face, and ran, uninvited into her mouth. She liked Thomas so much, it had been an effort to drag herself away. It was just as well she was leaving Oxford – she couldn't risk any further contact with him. Whatever would her grandfather say if he knew she had just spent the night with Thomas Kendal? He would have a fit! A heart attack, even. She must keep last night a secret – whatever the cost. A blush crept into her cheeks as she thought about the passionate night they had spent together.

Fliss wiped away her tears with her fingers. She hugged the little ginger cat. "Thank you, Thomas," she whispered to herself.

After Fliss's departure Thomas felt depressed. He made himself another coffee and sat at the kitchen table. He didn't feel like eating – he didn't feel like anything– he wanted to be with Fliss. He had loved everything about her. Her lovely face and figure, that flaming red hair, and magical green eyes. He loved her intelligence and sense of humour and the way she laughed – and now she was gone. He would probably never see her again.

Thomas sipped his coffee. He was restless and puzzled about his father. Why would Fliss's grandfather be so worried about his existance? What had his father been up to – to be watched by Special Branch? If his father had done something wrong – how could it possibly affect himself? He had never known his father – never had a chance to be influenced by him – it didn't make sense.

Perhaps it was something hereditary. Thomas knew nothing about his father's past. Perhaps his father had become insane. Thomas had a horrible vision of reaching the age of 30 and being carried off by men in white coats! He shuddered. That didn't make sense, either. If his father had become insane, his mother would have had him put into a good nursing home. No, that was rubbish, his father had still been a serving M.P. when he was shot. He couldn't have been mentally ill.

Thomas sat staring into his coffee cup. What sort of people did Special Branch deal with? Thomas froze – traitors! He suddenly smacked his hands down on the table. That had got to be it! His father could have been a Russian spy. Thomas knew nothing about his father's family – he could have been born in Russia and planted over here – married into the aristocracy, and got into parliament. He would have been in a perfect position to give away his country's secrets. It all made sense. His father was accidentally killed – his mother moved back to the Lake District – and the Russians, like Special Branch, didn't know that Thomas had been born!

Thomas's mind was racing. If the Russians knew about him, they might come after him. They could threaten or blackmail him into betraying his country when he eventually became an M.P. Why, he might even have family in Russia who would be killed if he didn't obey. Thomas's hands shook – there might even be people in the university who were watching him even now – they might already be his friends. He thought of Gus and Kal. "No!" he cried out loud. "NO! NO!" What was he going to do? There was no way he was going to be forced to betray his country.

Suddenly Thomas's mobile phone rang. It was lying on the table. Thomas stared at it in horror – picturing a member of the KGB at the other end! He picked up the phone with a trembling hand, and dropped it on the floor. "Hell!" he snapped as he picked it up, and put it to his ear.

"Thomas, are you there?" he heard his mother's voice.

"Yes, Mother," he stammered.

"Are you all right, Darling?" she queried.

"Yes, I'm fine," he replied nervously. "I...I...just got up."

"Well, you had better get a move on, Burrows is on his way to collect you. He'll be with you in a couple of hours."

"Don't worry, I'll be ready."

"Bye, Darling, see you later."

"Bye, Mother."

Thomas put down his phone and hurried off to the bathroom, to shave and shower and brush his teeth. When he was dressed he began to pack his bags for the journey home. As he was doing so, his doorbell rang. Thomas nearly jumped out of his skin! He had visions of two KGB men standing outside with their collars turned up and hats pulled over their eyes. He went to the intercom. "Who is it?" he asked sharply.

He heard Gus's voice.

"Tom, it's us, you idiot, open the door!"

Thomas breathed a sigh of relief, and released the catch. A couple of minutes later his two friends arrived. Thomas opened the door and let them in.

"What's up, Tom?" queried Gus, "you look like you've seen a ghost."

"Thomas, what is it, my friend, you do not look happy?" asked Kal, his brown eyes full of concern.

"I'm fine, chaps," replied Thomas, trying to sound cheerful. The three of them moved into the kitchen. Gus spotted the two coffee cups on the table.

"Oh, ho," he grinned. "What have we here, then?" he pointed to the two cups. "You've had a bird here, you lucky bastard!" Thomas blushed.

"I bet it was that slinky redhead!"

"Mind your own business, you four–eyed nosy parker!" grinned Thomas. They all laughed.

"Thomas, my friend, " interrupted Kal. "Please do not forget my invitation to come to my home in Portugal during the holidays. You may, of course, bring your mother, she would be most welcome." Thomas cringed.

"I can't promise, Kal, my mother...er...well... she doesn't like foreigners much, I'm afraid."

"You mean blacks," stated Gus, smoothing his hair and tightening the elastic band round his ponytail. Thomas looked uncomfortable.

"I'm sorry, Kal."

"That is alright, my friend, I understand," replied Kal gently.

"Well, we're off now, Tom. We only called in to say 'goodbye'" said Gus cheerfully.

"Thanks, chaps," replied Thomas, "see you both in October."

Gus and Kal left. Thomas watched them – Gus with his long legs almost dancing down the stairs, and Kal walking sedately behind him. Thomas closed the door behind them. He was thankful to be left alone. He needed time to think.

Thomas tidied the flat as well as he could, although someone would come in and give it a good clean before he returned. The flat was rather plain and bare compared with Westlake Manor. The walls were all plain with a few cheap watercolours on the walls. The living room had a cheap black leather suite and a glass coffee table on chrome legs. The only other furniture was a TV and a black wooden bookcase. The bedroom had a double bed and white fitted wardrobes and was decorated in black and white. The kitchen was large and well–fitted in shades of green, as was the bathroom.

By the time Burrows arrived, Thomas was ready. The chauffeur greeted him with a warm smile.

"Hello, there, young Thomas, it's good to see you."

"Thanks, Burrows, and how are you?"

"Fine thanks, and you?"

"Tired," grinned Thomas, "too many late nights!"

Burrows chuckled as he put Thomas's bags in the boot of the car.

"Well, you get a snooze in the back of the car. With me driving you'll sleep like a baby all the way home." Thomas laughed and climbed into the car. Burrows started up the car, the engine purred, and the car rolled smoothly away.

Thomas sat with his head back and closed his eyes. He didn't want to sleep – he just wanted to think. The first thing he needed to do was to discover as much as he could about his father's past, without his mother or grandparents knowing, just in case they were as ignorant as he had been. Or were they? His mother had wanted him to have a bodyguard in Oxford – did she suspect that he might be approached by Russians? His grandfather had stopped her – so he didn't know. Thomas's thoughts raced on. What if his mother did know? But if she did, she obviously wanted to keep quiet about it. He decided it would be safer if he, too, kept quiet.

Thomas hadn't a clue how to start tracing his father's ancestors. He would have to ask. He knew that his mother kept a scrap–book of newspaper cuttings about his father – he would start with those. He had seen them before, but he had not read them in any great depth. He decided that when he had done that, he would go to the local library and ask how to trace his ancestors. He would also look at the 'Who's Who' to see if his father was mentioned. It may give the names of his parents and where he was born.

Thomas did eventually fall asleep in the car, and didn't wake up until they drew up outside the large wrought iron gates leading up to the drive of Westlake Manor. Burrows pressed a button on a remote control, and the gates slid open.

When they got to the house Thomas was surrounded by people making a fuss of him. His mother and grandparents and staff were all pleased to see him.

"Well, Thomas," asked Marcus, "how have you enjoyed your first year at Oxford?"

"Great thanks, Grandfather, I've loved every minute of it."

"Good, good," replied Marcus nodding his head. Emma hugged her adored grandson.

"It's lovely to see you, dear." she cried happily. Joanna hugged her son, but had to complain.

"Thomas, just look at your hair – you will soon look like a girl – and those dreadful clothes!"

"Mother, don't fuss," replied Thomas frostily.

"Leave the lad alone, Joanna, he's only young once." scolded Marcus. Thomas smiled at his grandfather – a smile of thanks.

By the time Thomas had spoken to everyone and sorted out his bags it was mid–afternoon. The family sat in the drawing room drinking tea and eating carrot cake, Thomas's favourite, which had been made for him especially by the cook, Ellen.

After tea Joanna and Thomas went for a walk round their beautiful gardens. Joanna told Thomas that they were all going on holiday in two days time.

"Where are we going?" asked Thomas, suspiciously.

"We are flying down to Nice and joining Sebastian and his wife on their yacht – we shall be away for a month. We are also meeting up with the Beauchamp–Hill's." Thomas was furious.

"Mother," he snapped, "I am not going to marry Jemima Beauchamp–Hill. I've told you before, and now you expect me to have a month's holiday in her company!"

"Darling, don't be angry," soothed Joanna, putting on her 'sad' face. "Just be nice to her, she's a sweet girl."

"Mother, she may be pretty and sweet, but she's brainless!"

"Thomas," argued his mother, "please don't be unkind, you hurt me so." Thomas sighed.

"I wanted to go over to Portugal and stay with my friend, Kal and his family – they have invited me." Joanna's eyes hardened.

"Kal, what kind of a name is that?" Thomas grew uneasy.

"I told you, he's Portuguese." he replied warily.

"No doubt he is if he comes from Portugal," his mother snapped. "I hope he's not black!" Thomas felt his confidence slowly disappear.

"He's...a...a...half-caste," stammered Thomas. Joanna's eyes turned to chips of ice.

"In other words, he's black," she stormed. Thomas felt angry and clenched his fists.

"Well, I don't care, he's my friend and I like him," he answered, his voice growing hard. Joanna glared at him.

"Thomas, I will not have you mixing with blacks – I've told you before."

"Why not?" stormed Thomas. He was getting more angry. "How can you not like them? My father did. He used to help them. He even put some of his own money into making homes for third world refugees – you don't make any sense!"

"Don't be so stupid, Thomas, " she was shouting at him now. Your father hated blacks as much as I did."

"How could he?" stormed Thomas, "he was a Member of Parliament, he was good and honest."

"Exactly!" snapped his mother, "if he had been honest about his views he would have been thrown out of office!" Thomas was stunned.

"So he lied?"

"Of course, Thomas, all politicians have to lie, don't be so naive!" Thomas was too shocked to speak.

"Thomas, you are coming to Nice with us, and that's final!" his mother stated angrily. Her voice was as hard as steel. She turned swiftly, and marched back to the house.

Thomas stood as if turned to stone and stared in disbelief at his mother's retreating back. He had had two shocks about his father in a matter of hours. He couldn't believe it. The idol of his dead father was crumbling at his feet...

If his father had lied about liking black people, he may have lied about his other beliefs. His father could have been a "right bastard" he thought bitterly.

Thomas walked alone through the grounds, deeply unhappy. He did not like arguing with his mother, but he was growing to dislike her. She was an utter snob, spiteful and cruel, and it looked very much as though his father may have been the same.

Thomas hardly spoke to his mother during their four-week cruise. They had all arrived in Nice where the weather had been glorious. Thomas liked Nice – the beautiful villas set on the white cliffs, and the streets lined with palm trees, the magnificent hotels and the blue, blue sea.

They boarded the luxury yacht of Sebastian Luke, a well-known film star. Many years ago Marcus had financed a successful film for Sebastian, and they had remained friends ever since.

They did have a good holiday – cruising the Mediterranean and calling in at different places. Thomas did his best to avoid the silly, chattering Jemima, but out of politeness he was never rude to her. His grandparents noticed the coolness between him and his mother, they let him know, tactfully, that they knew and understood. Thomas was grateful to them both.

They got back to Westlake Manor, relaxed and sun-tanned. It was August and the weather was good. Thomas went horse riding and visited Tim, the backward son of the gardener. Tim was as tall as Thomas. He had grown into a hard–working young man. He was still quiet – and had a vacant look in his eyes, which lit up at the sight of Thomas. Thomas patted Tim on the back, who took his arm and dragged him off to their cottage where he was welcomed by Ben and his wife, who made a great fuss of him. Thomas envied them their quaint little home and their simple, uncomplicated lives.

As soon as Thomas had the opportunity he was going to go through the newspaper cuttings of his father. One day his mother had gone out for the whole day with a friend, and his grandparents had gone out to do some shopping in one of the nearby towns. Although Emma did most of her shopping through the Internet, she liked nothing better than wandering round the shops for new clothes.

Thomas fetched the scrapbook from his mother's room and took it to his own room. He sat propped up against the pillows and slowly turned the pages. There were many articles and photos of his father. They showed Thomas Kendal snr. at the openings of homes and shelters for third world refugees, crippled children and the homeless and down-and-outs. His father was there, blond and handsome, smiling and shaking hands with people. Thomas was deeply hurt that a lot of his father's good deeds were possibly a facade. He read the articles carefully, but there was nothing to give him a clue, and no mention of Russians! When Thomas got to the last few pages, he frowned. There were many pictures and articles about his father's murder and funeral, but there were pieces deliberately cut out. What was his mother hiding? What was it she did not want him to see?

Thomas got off the bed and went to look out of the window, he was getting nowhere trying to solve this mystery. He watched Marcus and Emma arrive home, so picked up the scrapbook, sneaked along the wide landing and hastily replaced it in his mother's room.

He went back to his own room, still frowning. He needed to get hold of some newspapers from 1991 so that he could see the articles about his father's funeral, to see what his mother had removed. He decided he would go to the local library.

One thing that Thomas liked about being at home was that he was able to use his car. The quiet towns and villages that nestled in the Lake District did not have the car restrictions like the big cities. Thomas's car had been a gift from Marcus and Emma on his eighteenth birthday. It was a sleek red Jaguar, the latest model. It boasted a computer with a navigation system, which would also tell him if there was a hold–up ahead and give him an alternate route. It also gave him car–park information and the times of trains and planes. It had a voice–activated telephone and infrared lights for foggy weather. Thomas loved his car!

The next day Thomas drove into town, parked his car and walked into the library. As soon as Thomas walked in people he knew met him. He was horrified. He had not given a thought to the fact that his family was well known in the area. There was no way he could do any research here – the whole of the Lake District would know about it! He would just have to wait until he got back to Oxford.

Weeks of boredom and frustration lay ahead for Thomas. He was not due back at Oxford until 1st October. In desperation he rang Kal in Portugal to ask if he could go and visit. His friend was more than pleased. Thomas told his mother – who was less than pleased!

A few days later Thomas set off for Portugal. He arrived at Kal's home, an enormous villa on the Vivenda dos Arcos in the beautiful town of Estoril. Estoril was the Portuguese Riviera, twenty miles from Lisbon. There were excellent sporting facilities such as golf, fishing, water-skiing, sailing and horse riding. The scenery was breathtaking with picturesque walks and parks, grand homes and gardens, and a magnificent yacht club in the 'olde worlde' harbour which was full of colourful boats. The streets were cobbled and filled with shops of arts and crafts, and top class restaurants. There was also a huge casino on top of a hill amongst the palm trees. The gaming was room was famous for it's first class shows. The river Tagus ran through this lovely place, like a glistening ribbon.

Thomas liked Kal's family. His father, Alexandre, was a lawyer, as was his older brother Luis Alvez. His sister, Maria was a sweet and shy girl, much younger than Kal. Kal's mother was an Indian, called Yasmin. She was small and petite with melting brown eyes like her son, and long black hair that hung down her back like a shining curtain. Thomas thought she was beautiful.

Thomas had a wonderful holiday, and was made so welcome by the D'Sara's. They were all fascinated by his blue eyes and golden hair. Thomas and his friend went horse riding and sailing and swimming and sightseeing in this beautiful country. Thomas felt happy and relaxed.

He returned to the Lake District towards the end of September.

It was almost time to go back to Oxford – and to start tracing his father's family tree.

CHAPTER FOUR

A SHOCK FOR THOMAS - OCTOBER 2011

Thomas returned to Oxford with mixed feelings. He was glad to be away from his mother, but at the same time was uneasy about being at university where everyone knew who he was. He was afraid in case he was being followed by the Russians, or being watched by the Special Branch. Fliss's grandfather, Andrew Shaw, could easily have contacted Special Branch – they may be watching his every move. Thomas was scared.

The start of the new term had been a hive of activity. There had been much backslapping and laughter and chatter when everyone met up after the long summer break. Thomas, Gus and Kal, as usual went everywhere together. Thomas felt safer. He badly wanted to go to the local library to check the newspapers, and to ask how to start tracing his ancestors, but he was afraid in case he was being followed. He felt lost and lonely.

Thomas had been back at Oxford for two weeks. It was a warm, sunny afternoon, and Gus and Kal had gone to the cinema with a couple of girls to see the latest science fiction film. Thomas didn't like science fiction and didn't want to go. He suddenly found himself alone, so he decided to go to the Oxford Central Library in the Westgate shopping centre.

He set off, looking handsome in black jeans and polo neck sweater, but his tanned face was lined with worry, and his blue eyes clouded and anxious.

He walked along Keble Street, and turned left and made his way along until he came into Cornmarket Street, which was crowded with shoppers and students. His mind elsewhere, he did not look where he was going. Suddenly he bumped into a girl. "I'm sorry," he exclaimed.

"That's OK," replied the girl. Thomas looked down to see a small girl with merry brown eyes, a humorous mouth and a head of shining brown curls.

"It's my fault," apologised Thomas, "I wasn't looking where I was going." The girl looked at him and frowned.

"Aren't you Thomas Kendal?" she asked.

"Yes, I am," he replied with a smile.

"The one whose father was an M.P. and got shot?"

"Yes, I am," he replied.

"Oh!" she exclaimed. "I live next door to your grandparents." Thomas laughed and scratched the back of his head.

"No–one lives next door to my grandparents," he smiled, thinking of the isolation of Westlake Manor.

"I don't mean your mother's parents, I mean your father's." At this moment a tall girl with glasses came up and grabbed her arm and pulled her away.

"Come on, Sally" she cried.

Thomas stood as if turned to stone – the blood drained from his face. He leaned against a shop window feeling faint. An old lady stopped and patted his arm. "Are you alright, dear?" she asked

"Yes...yes...thank you," he stammered.

Thomas was so shocked he could hardly breathe. He rubbed a hand over his chest, and took deep breaths. What did that girl mean? He hadn't got any other grandparents – had he? Thomas suddenly realised that the girl had gone. He had to speak to her! He started to panic. What if she was only here for a day as a visitor, and not a student? He had to find her!

Thomas pushed his way between the crowds of people, his heart pounding. He looked in every shop he passed, but there was no sign of her. "I must find her...I must find her," he kept saying to himself.

Eventually Thomas came to a pub, he ran inside and stopped. She was there sitting with a crowd of obvious students. Taking a deep breath he walked over to her and gently tapped her on the shoulder.

"Excuse me, but could I speak to you for a moment?" The girl turned round and looked into Thomas's ashen face.

"Of course," she replied, patting the seat next to her.

"In private," he said huskily.

"OK," Thomas gripped her arm and guided her through the pub into the garden at the back. They sat at a wooden table in the far corner. Thomas looked hard at her.

"What did you mean about knowing my grandparents?"

"I live next door to them," she answered, puzzled.

"Who are they...what are they like...where are they?" he stammered. She looked into his puzzled eyes.

"You don't know about them do you?" she asked in amazement.

"No," he replied, shaking his head.

"They don't know about you either." Thomas and the girl stared at each other in silence. A silence that was almost a sound.

"Please tell me," he begged, leaning over the table – his face close to hers.

"Well," she began. "Your grandfather is Henry Kendal...he's about 70...he's a retired school teacher. Your grandmother is Penny...she's about 70, too. I understand she was heartbroken when your father died." Thomas's stomach was churning.

"What are they like?" he urged. The girl swallowed hard – she felt uncomfortable at Thomas's distress.

"Your grandfather is a lovely man...he's kind and gentle and very clever. Penny is small, dumpy and motherly...she would have loved grandchildren, but she's never had any..."

"Did you know my father?" he asked.

"No," she replied. "He died before I was born. I was born later after Amy got married."

"Amy?" queried Thomas.

"Your father's sister."

"Good God!" exclaimed Thomas," I have grandparents and an aunt! I can hardly believe it."

"How come you didn't know?" she asked.

"My mother told me my father's family were dead," he replied in a strangled whisper. "I'll never forgive her, never!"

"She must be pretty awful," stated the girl.

"She is." Thomas, by now, was shaking with anger. He clenched his hands together to stop their trembling. The girl touched his arm.

"Thomas, are you alright?" He lifted his head and looked across at her.

"Yes, – I'm just getting over the shock – thanks. By the way, who are you?"

"My name's Sally Bennett," she smiled.

"Hello, Sally," smiled Thomas weakly, "where are you from?"

"I live in Cropwell."

"Where's that?"

"It's a small market town on the borders of Leicestershire and Warwickshire – it's very pretty." Thomas nodded, slowly.

"Was my father adopted?" asked Thomas suddenly, the two KGB men were slowly disappearing out of his mind.

"Adopted? I don't think so," she replied slowly.

"My father's sister, Amy – what is she like?"

"Oh, she's lovely," exclaimed Sally. "She's slim and pretty with fair hair and blue eyes. She's about forty-five – married to Joel. He's a bank manager in Melton Mowbray. They live there in a great big house during the week, and at the weekends they stay in her cottage in Bishops Fell. She inherited it from her grandmother Kendal before your father died."

"Do you like my family, Sally?"

"Very much," she replied. "They are lovely people. I was in Henry's class at school when I was younger. We all loved him. He just seems to have the skill of making people feel good, even if they aren't very clever."

"They sound wonderful," whispered Thomas.

"Would you like to meet them, Thomas?" asked Sally. He was taken aback at this suggestion.

"I...I'm not sure. They may be angry."

"I'm sure they won't be angry with you, Thomas. They might want to kill your mother, though," she smiled.

"I wouldn't blame them," replied Thomas. "Look, Sally, I would love to meet them, but I just need to get used to the idea first."

"That's OK Thomas. Just let me know when you are ready, and I'll ask my mum to go round and tell them." Thomas began to brighten up a little.

"Do you have a photo of my family?" he asked.

"No, but I can get you one. My parents went to Amy's wedding, and they have lots of photos of Amy and your parents. I'll ask my mum to send me a nice one."

"Thank you, Sally." A smile was creeping back into his eyes.

"Is there anything else I can do to help?"

"Yes," replied Thomas, "there is. Can you come to the library with me? I was on my way there when I bumped into you. I was going to ask about tracing my ancestors, and I want to check up on some old newspapers about my father's life and death. My mother has got some cuttings, but pieces have been cut out."

"Of course I'll come with you. I'll just have to let my friends know." They both stood up and walked back into the pub, where Sally told her friends she would meet up with them later.

Thomas and Sally set off for the library, her brown curls bobbing about as she walked along. They arrived at the library and went to the enquiry desk, where they were told to go up to the second floor to the local studies, which was now open six days a week. They climbed the stairs together. Thomas's stomach was churning again – what was he going to find?

Thomas and Sally walked up to the enquiry desk where a pleasant, middle-aged lady wearing glasses, spoke to them.

"Can I help you?" she asked brightly.

"Yes, please. Could you tell me how I could find my father's birth certificate?"

"Oh, yes," she replied, "we have all the birth, marriage and death registrations up to the year 2000 on computer."

"Here?" gasped Thomas.

"Oh, yes, what year are you looking for?" Thomas and Sally looked at each other.

"Er... about 1960," replied Thomas.

"That's no problem. You will need to fill in this form first, with your name and address. Are you a student?" she asked. Thomas nodded. "Can you make sure you tick the student column?" she asked politely. Thomas filled in the form and gave it to her. She then went to a box behind her and lifted out a red floppy disc. She smiled.

"Red for births, green for marriages and black for deaths – same as the certificates. Come with me." Thomas and Sally followed the lady to a row of computers – many of them in use. She told them to pick a computer and sit down, which they did, Sally fetching another chair. The lady slipped the disc into the machine.

"It's all very simple," she explained. "You press the enter button to bring up the menu, then you type in the year where it says 'year', then the quarter where it says 'quarter'."

"Quarter?" asked Thomas. The lady went on to explain.

"The years are divided into four quarters – March, June, September and December. For example if your father was born in January – his name would be in the March quarter – there are three months in each quarter. The only information you will get in the register is the name of the person, the place where they were registered, and a reference number. The year you are looking for will have the mother's maiden name at the side, but as you get much further back, it won't."

Thomas typed in 1960 and then tried the March quarter.

"Now type in your surname." Thomas typed in the name KENDAL, pressed the 'enter' button, and suddenly the screen was filled with Kendals.

"If it's not there, " continued the lady, "just press the 'escape' button and you will be back to the main menu – you just start again. You press the 'arrow' keys for going up and down the pages."

"Thank you," smiled Thomas. The lady walked away to see to another customer.

Thomas and Sally stared at the screen. All the Kendals were in alphabetical order. He moved the screen down until he got to the 'T's, but there was no Thomas Kendal registered in Cropwell.

"Are you sure my father was born in Cropwell?" he asked Sally.

"I think so," she replied with a frown. There was no trace of Thomas Kendal snr. in any of the quarters for 1960, so they went on to 1961. His name wasn't in the March quarter, so they went on to June. Suddenly Sally whispered excitedly.

"There he is – Thomas Kendal – mother – Hall – Cropwell!"

"Was my grandmother's maiden name Hall?"

"I don't know, " replied Sally shaking her head. "Shall we look for Henry's and Penny's marriage – then we'll know?"

"Brilliant idea!" cried Thomas, happily. "Let's write these details down first." He fished a folded sheet of paper out of his pocket, which he had brought with him in readiness, and a pen. He wrote down the details, and Sally took the 'births' disc back and returned with a green 'marriage' disc.

"The lady said that each marriage partner's name will be on this, beside each other, and also each person will be listed separately in the register, with the same reference number – so we will have to check Kendal and Hall."

"Right, " said Thomas slipping the disc into the machine. "Where shall we start?"

"Well, if your father was born in 1961 – let's try 1960 and work backwards," she suggested. They sat together, their eyes glued to the screen. They soon found a Henry Kendal married in Cropwell to a Hall in the October quarter of 1960. Thomas's eyes lit up.

"Now let's look for a Penny Hall," whispered Thomas.

"Yes!" cried out Sally – and there it was, Penelope Hall – Kendall – Cropwell – and the same reference number. Thomas and Sally looked at each and smiled.

"Let's see if we can find Henry's birth," suggested Thomas. Sally went off again, and came back with another 'birth' disc which included the 1940's.

They searched through many registers for the birth of Henry Kendal, but there were none in Cropwell. "That's strange," murmured Thomas, "could he have been born somewhere else?" Sally suddenly gasped, then covered her mouth with her hand.

"What's the matter, Sally?"

"I've just remembered!"

"What is it?"

"My mum told me something years ago about Henry. Apparently one day, I think it was when Amy was on her honeymoon, a woman turned up at Henry's house claiming she was his sister. It seems that they had been born in another country and got separated. It was all very exciting. She was older than Henry, and she died a few years ago." Thomas felt a cold knot form in his stomach.

"Where was he born, Sally?" urged Thomas.

"I'm not sure – but it was somewhere unfriendly like Russia or Germany."

Thomas felt sick. The two KGB men had just crept back into his head.

"Thomas, are you OK?" asked Sally anxiously. Thomas nodded.

"Do you want to look at the newspapers now?" Thomas looked up.

"Yes, of course."

They took the disc back to the desk, and asked the lady how he could order the certificates of his father's birth and his grandparent's marriage.

"You can order them through the Internet, as long as you have a credit card."

"I'd like to do that, please," he replied. The lady took him back to the computer and showed Thomas how to order the certificates direct from the registry office in Southport, and told him to expect them within the week.

"Do you have records of old newspapers?" asked Thomas

"Yes, we do."

"Do you have the Daily Telegraph?"

"Yes, we have them on computer from the year 1998."

"Do you not have them for 1991?"

"No, I'm afraid not. We only have our local paper, and that is on microfilm. Will that be any good?"

"Yes, please, we'll try that. Do you have 1991 and the two previous years?"

"Yes. It will take me a few minutes to get them. Would you like to take a seat?"

Thomas and Sally sat and waited. Thomas looked round the library – he still wondered if he was being followed. He watched the library staff helping many people.

"It looks as if there are a lot of people tracing their ancestors," he remarked to Sally.

"That's just what I was thinking," she replied.

The lady with the glasses approached them.

"Please follow me." They followed her to another row of machines. They were large with big screens. She fitted the film into a machine, and Thomas watched carefully.

"Each film contains one year of papers. I've put 1991 on for you. The button on your right is forward, the one on your left is to wind back. The further round you turn the buttons, the faster the film will move. If you want photocopies you will need fifty pence pieces. You put them in this slot and press the green button."

"Thank you very much," Thomas and Sally replied in unison.

Thomas fast–forwarded the film to the end of March and then slowly wound it back until he found the funeral of his father. There was a large picture of him with an article underneath. He put in a 50p, pressed the button and after a few kicks and rumbles a copy fell into the tray. Thomas and Sally sat in silence whilst the film rolled back slowly. They came across another picture. It was a group of people climbing the steps of a house. They were all dressed in black, a few flakes of snow falling about them. Sally touched Thomas's arm.

"There's your grandparents, Thomas."

"What!" he gasped. Sally pointed to a man of medium height with light hair, wearing glasses. The collar of his coat turned up.

"That's Henry," she spoke quietly, "and next to him is Penny."

Thomas looked at the woman next to his grandfather. She was shorter than Henry – dressed in black with some sort of dark woolly hat pulled over her head. She held a handkerchief to her eyes as though she was crying. Thomas was filled with emotion at this crying woman – his father's own mother – a heartbroken mother.

"God!" he whispered, "how could my mother not tell this poor woman about me? How could my mother's parents condone such a thing?" He looked at Sally, dazedly. "I just can't believe it!"

Thomas stared and stared at the picture in sheer disbelief. Eventually he asked Sally, "who are these other people?"

"The girl in the black hooded coat is Amy, and the man next to her is Joel." she replied. Thomas put in his fifty pence and pressed the 'print' button and waited for the copy to drop in to the tray. He picked it up and gazed at it for a moment, then put it back into the tray.

When Thomas finally gained control of his emotions he continued. There were a number of articles about his father's death, including a picture of Kendrick House, where his father had been shot. Thomas took photocopies of everything, after changing some money into a pile of fifty p's.

As the film was winding back, Thomas suddenly frowned and stopped.

"What's wrong?" asked Sally.

"This Kendrick House – I've seen a mention of that place between my father's death and his funeral." Thomas moved the film on again – and there it was – "Mystery Deaths at Kendrick House." The article went on to say that a number of drug addicts who were being treated at the clinic had been found dead. Thomas pressed the 'print' button and whilst waiting for the copy he frowned at Sally.

"I wonder if the person who killed my father also killed these people?"

"It's certainly a coincidence," she replied, mystified.

When the copy dropped into the tray Thomas moved the film on again. "Here we are!" he smiled grimly.

"Look," said Sally, "there it is." They skimmed through the article. It reported that the drugs given to the patients had been poisoned.

"Bloody hell!" cried Thomas. He printed off a copy, and wound the film back. Thomas finished the film for 1991, and put in 1990. He started in January and moved on. They found a lot of articles about Thomas's father and pictures of him at the openings of homes for third–world refugees, crippled children and the homeless.

As they were going through the film Sally suddenly asked Thomas to stop.

"What's up?"

“That home for the refugees that was burnt down, we've just passed – I'm sure your father was at the opening.” Thomas wound the film back.

“You're right,” he replied. “That's two occasions when my father has opened a home and there's been a tragedy – I wonder if someone was trying to destroy him?”

“Let's check the rest,” suggested Sally.

They checked the rest of the film, taking copies of everything. They had found more incidents of a similar nature. The worst they found was a home of crippled children who had all been gassed by a faulty heating system.

“This is awful,” muttered Thomas in a low voice. He was beginning to wonder if the Special Branch had been following his father to protect him – perhaps he had been in danger?”

A member of staff came over to them to say that the library was due to close. Thomas and Sally handed over the films and left the library.

When they got outside the library, they both shivered. The sun had disappeared behind grey, scurrying clouds, and it was getting dark. Sally's brown curls were dancing in the breeze.

Thomas looked down at her. “Sally, I can't thank you enough for what you've done for me today.”

“That's OK Thomas,” she smiled, “It was a pleasure.”

“Let me take you for something to eat. What do you fancy?”

“I'd love a pizza, salad and garlic bread.”

“Sounds marvellous. Come on!” The two of them set off down the nearest street and soon came across a Pizza restaurant, which was already half full. They found a seat and settled themselves and picked up a menu. The restaurant was clean and modern, consisting of much glass and shiny metal poles and chairs. A waitress came over and Thomas ordered a bottle of white wine, whilst they searched the huge menu. By the time the wine arrived they were ready to order.

Thomas poured their wine and they chatted quietly about all that had happened that day. Thomas was desperate to confide in someone. After their meal Thomas decided to confide in Sally, and told her what Fliss had told him about his father and of the row he had had with his mother. "What do you think, Sally?" he asked her urgently.

"Well," she replied carefully, "I must agree that if your father was doing something wrong, it can't possibly affect you. I doubt if he was going insane, Henry and Penny are perfectly all right, and I'm sure they would have known if there was something wrong with him. I think you must be right about him being a traitor – that would explain the Special Branch angle. He could have been forced into it, and maybe the same people will try it with you – but it does seem a bit far–fetched."

"I know, but I've made a decision."

"What's that?" she answered, eyebrows raised.

"I won't go into politics," he replied simply. "If I'm not in a position to have state secrets or information, I can't pass them on, can I?"

"Of course, not," she smiled. "That's a good idea, Thomas."

"I could easily do something else – there are plenty of other careers. By the way, Sally, what are you studying?"

"Languages." Thomas's heart skipped a beat – she was studying the same subject as Fliss.

"What do you want to do when you leave Oxford?" he asked, hoping she wouldn't say she was going to work for Shaw's travel agency.

"I don't know, yet. I might decide to work abroad as a translator for a while, and then maybe come back to England to teach. I just haven't decided."

They discussed Thomas's problem for a little while longer, then Thomas paid the bill and they left the warmth of the restaurant to meet a chilly wind. It was dark and cold. Thomas and Sally hurried towards Keble. Sally shared a flat with two other girls. He walked her to her door, and before going in she promised to phone her mother to ask for the photograph for Thomas.

Thomas returned to his own flat, clutching his precious photocopies to his chest. Thomas was glad that he could afford a flat to himself – it was now giving him the privacy he needed. He let himself in – fetched a couple of cans of lager from the fridge and went into the sitting room. He switched on the TV for company, keeping the sound low, switched on the table lamp and the electric fire to make the room look warm and comfortable. He settled himself on the settee, the cans of lager perched on the arm, and, in an act of defiance against his mother, plonked his feet on the coffee table. He switched off his mobile phone and began to read the newspaper cuttings.

Most of them were similar to the one's his mother had at home. The ones she didn't have were the tragic deaths of the people in some of the homes where his father had been at the openings, and the pictures of his family at his funeral. His mother had, obviously, not wanted him to know about them. How could she have been so cruel? Thomas's eyes kept wandering to the picture of his Kendal family climbing those steps in the snow, and of his grandmother, Penny, crying. Thomas was a caring and sensitive person and was deeply hurt by Penny's distress. How would she feel when she knew that she had a twenty-year-old grandson? He read the article again, which described his father's family, and was deeply touched by Henry's reply of, "we're too upset to talk to anyone," when approached by reporters.

Thomas sat for a long time reading the newspaper cuttings, but could still not find an answer. He eventually went to bed. He lay there listening to the wind, now roaring outside the window, and the rain spattering against the window. He slept fitfully, dreaming about Henry and Penny and Amy who were being followed by two KGB men with their turned up collars, and hats tilted over their eyes, who, in turn, were being followed by men in white coats! Then there were visions of Fliss with her waterfall of red hair and Sally with her brown curls dancing round her heart-shaped face and tickling her neck, and ghosts floating through swirling snow.

By the time Thomas had got up and had some breakfast, Gus and Kal were at his door.

"Where were you last night?" demanded Gus. Thomas felt uncomfortable.

"I went to the library to do some work, and I didn't feel like going out when I got back." He didn't tell his friends about Sally or the Kendals. The three lads spent the day together.

The following Wednesday morning Thomas got up and dressed and went down to check his post. He opened the box, and his eyes lit up and the sight of an envelope with a Southport postmark. He raced up the stairs two at a time, and let himself back into his flat. He tore open the envelope, which revealed the two certificates.

Thomas sat at the kitchen table and stared at the two certificates. The top one was his grandparent's marriage. Henry Kendal–19 years–bachelor–student – Father Henry Kendal (deceased) a soldier. The address was Jade Cottage, Bishops Fell. His grandmother was Penelope Hall – nineteen years – spinster – typist – Father Richard Hall, a fireman. Her address was 14, Belvoir Road, Cropwell. The marriage took place on 3rd November, 1961. The witnesses were Caroline Kendal, presumably Henry's mother, and Richard Hall, Penny's father.

The second certificate was his father's birth. Thomas Kendal born 8th May, 1962 at the General Hospital, Cropwell. His father was Henry Kendal, a student and Penelope Kendal, formerly Hall. The birth was registered by Penny – address 14, Belvoir Road, Cropwell.

It was obvious that Henry had got Penny pregnant, which was why they had married so young. It was also clear that Penny was living with her parents, whilst Henry was away at college or university somewhere. Thomas also realised, with relief, that his father could not have been adopted. The two KGB men in his head finally waved goodbye.

Whilst Thomas was gazing at the certificates, his mobile phone rang. It was Sally.

"Hi, Thomas, I've got the photo you wanted, it's just arrived."

"That's brilliant, Sally, so have the certificates."

"That's great. Would you like me to bring the photo round?"

"Yes, please. Come round now and I'll make you some toast and coffee. It's about all I can manage."

"I'm on my way," she laughed.

By the time Sally arrived Thomas had a plate of hot, buttered toast and two mugs of coffee ready. He let her in and took her into the kitchen, and sat her at the table. She handed Thomas the photograph, and he passed her the certificates. Sally tucked into the toast as she read them. "Mmm... I'm famished," she stated happily.

Thomas gazed at the photo of Amy's wedding, his blue eyes moving slowly from face to face. The men all looked handsome in their grey morning suits. He recognised Henry from the newspaper article. Quite tall, with fair, thinning hair and gold rimmed glasses. His face was aquiline, with a warm smile. Penny was shorter, and looked pretty in a lovely blue suit and matching hat, her shining, brown hair peeping beneath the brim. She looked happy and proud. The bride, his Aunt Amy, looked beautiful.

She was wearing a white dress with layers of frills. Her fair hair was adorned with strands of pearls. She had blue eyes. a small nose and mouth, like her mother , and even white teeth. Beside her was Joel, who was also quite tall and broad-shouldered. He had dark hair and eyes, and also wore glasses. His skin looked swarthy like that of the attractive–looking woman dressed in yellow – clearly his mother. Joel's father was tall and well–built, like a rugger player.

"Thomas, eat up!" Sally patted his arm.

"Sorry, I was miles away. This photo is really good. May I keep it?"

"Of course," she smiled. "I'll have to go now, Thomas. Thanks for the breakfast." Thomas stood up.

"Sally...I...think...I...would like to meet my grandparents, now...can you...?"

"Of course. I'll ring my mum tonight and ask her to go round and tell them. When would you like to go – this weekend?"

"Yes, please," he answered nervously.

"OK, I'll ring you when I've fixed it up."

"Thanks, Sally, I'll see you later."

When Sally had gone, Thomas sat and finished his coffee – still gazing at the photo – and still amazed at all that had happened since he had arrived in Oxford.

On impulse he picked up the photo and the keys to his flat, and hurried along to the local shops to buy a frame for the photo. The assistant was very helpful, and when Thomas had chosen an expensive wooden frame with a gold trim, she fitted the photo into it for him

"Your family?" she asked.

"Yes," he replied, proudly.

As Thomas returned to his flat he was met by Gus and Kal.

"What have you got there, Tom?" asked Gus.

"Come on up and I'll show you," he replied shortly.

The three lads walked into the kitchen.

"Thomas, my friend, what is wrong? You are not looking as yourself lately," frowned Kal. Thomas looked at his two friends.

"I've had a bit of a shock, fellas."

"Go on, Tom, spit it out!" Thomas felt rather shy.

"Last Saturday, when you two were at the pictures, I was in Cornmarket Street when I bumped into a girl called Sally. She asked me if I was Thomas Kendal, and when I said I was, she said she lived next door to my grandparents."

"The Westlakes?" asked Gus, puzzled.

"No, the Kendals," replied Thomas.

"What!" shouted Gus. "I thought they were dead."

"So did I," replied Thomas," but they're not. They live in a place called Cropwell – where my father was born."

"I do not understand, Thomas. How can this be?" asked Kal, totally confused.

"My mother told me they were dead... I also have an aunt, my father's sister."

"Bloody hell, Tom. Your mother's a right old cow – how could she have done that?"

"I don't know. I can't understand her at all," stammered Thomas," but I've got a photo that Sally' mother has sent." He passed them the photo. Gus and Kal stared at it for some time.

"Wow!" whispered Gus. "This bride looks a bit of alright!"

"That's my Aunt Amy, she got married after my father died – these are my grandparents, that's Joel, and the other couple are his parents."

"What are you going to do, Tom?" asked Gus.

"Sally is going to ask her parents to go round and tell them about me. If they want to see me I'll go down this weekend."

"Are you going to tell your mother, Tom?" asked Gus through narrowed eyes.

"No bloody fear!" snapped Thomas.

“We will say nothing, Thomas,” added Kal earnestly. “You must tell us all about them when you meet.”

Thomas looked at his watch. “Time to go, chaps.” He put down the photo in the living room and picked up his books, and the three of them set off for their lecture, talking quietly about Thomas’s discovery.

CHAPTER FIVE

THOMAS MEETS THE KENDALS - NOVEMBER 2010

Henry and Penny Kendal were sitting by their gas fire. They were warm and relaxed – Henry sitting in his favourite armchair with his feet upon a stool, his newspaper resting on his lap whilst he was watching the news. Penny was snuggled down on the settee, glasses perched on the end of her nose reading a romantic novel. She would be glad when the news was over so that she could see the next episode of Coronation Street. The day had been grey, cold and windy, and they were both glad to be indoors.

Suddenly they heard the front door bell ringing. "Who on earth can that be on a night like this?" asked Henry.

"I'll go and see," grumbled Penny, easing herself from her comfortable seat and trotting off to the front door. When she opened it she found her next–door neighbours, Richard and Molly Bennett, standing in the porch.

"Hello, Penny, can we have a word?" asked Molly softly.

"Of course," replied Penny smiling. "Come in and make your selves at home." The three of them moved into the cosy living room and sat down, Molly next to Penny on the settee and Richard in the other armchair. Henry looked across at Richard.

"What's up, Richard? I can see something's bothering you." Molly and Richard looked across at each other.

"We've got something to tell you both. It's going to be a bit of a shock," stated Molly breathlessly. Henry looked across at Molly, his expression gentle.

"Just take your time, Molly." He spoke kindly.

Molly sat twisting her fingers in her lap. She took a deep breath. "Well, you know our Sally is at Oxford?" Henry and Penny nodded.

"Er...well…she's met a young man there, a couple of years older than her. His name is...Thomas Kendal..." There was a complete silence. Henry eventually spoke up.

"What are you trying to tell us, Molly?" She looked across at Henry.

"He's your grandson," she replied. Henry sat up and frowned.

"Are you quite sure?" he asked gently.

"Oh, yes," she replied," he comes from the Lake District – his mother's name is Joanna – and he says he is the son of Thomas Kendal, the M.P."

"Good God!" cried Henry. Penny turned as white as a sheet, and started to shake. Molly took hold of her hands and rubbed them between her own.

"A grandson! I can't believe it!" she whispered.

"It's true, Penny," said Molly softly. Penny started to cry. She lay her head on Molly's shoulder and sobbed.

Henry rubbed a hand over his head. "This is incredible," he murmured. "What is he like, Molly?"

"Well, according to Sally he's very nice. He's tall and blond with blue eyes."

"Why did he never contact us?" wept Penny, her eyes now turning red, her face blotched.

"He didn't know about you until he met Sally," explained Molly quietly.

"What!" stormed Henry, "he didn't know?"

Penny raised her tear-stained face in anger. "That bitch, Joanna. She had a child and kept him a secret! And Emma and Marcus – why didn't they tell us? How could they be so cruel?" Penny by now was distraught and kept shaking her head in disbelief.

"Do you know when he was born, Molly?" asked Henry, still unable to believe what he had heard.

"Yes," replied Molly, "eight months after Thomas died."

"So, she was pregnant at his funeral," stated Henry slowly, nodding his head. Richard now spoke up.

"Henry, Thomas would like to come and see you both." Henry and Penny looked straight at Richard.

"Oh," gasped Penny, "Yes...yes... we'd love to see him!"

"Indeed we would," added Henry, choked.

"This is Thomas's mobile number – he's waiting for you to call."

Meanwhile Thomas and Sally were sitting in Thomas's kitchen. They had eaten a Chinese take-away – and were now drinking a bottle of wine. Thomas looked at the empty tinfoil dishes scattered on the table.

"They still haven't rung," he said, sadly.

"I've told you, Thomas," Sally replied gently, "my parents still go to work, they're a bit younger than Henry and Penny. I didn't tell my mum until six o'clock tonight."

"I'm sorry, Sally, I'm all on edge."

"It's OK, Thomas, I understand."

Thomas's mobile suddenly rang. They both jumped in alarm. With a shaking hand Thomas picked up his mobile and spoke into it. "Hello."

"Am I speaking to Thomas Kendal?" asked a quiet, well–spoken voice.

"Y...yes."

"I am Henry Kendal. I understand you are my grandson, and would like to come and see us?"

"Yes...yes...I would..."

"You would be most welcome, Thomas, we would like to meet you very much, too. When would you like to come down?"

"Would this weekend be alright?" he asked nervously.

"Certainly. How about coming down on Friday after lectures, and staying until Sunday?"

"That would be marvellous – I'll come down with Sally, and she can show me where you live."

"Excellent idea. Is there anything special you would like to do whilst you are here?"

"I...don't mind. I'll do whatever you wish."

"Thomas, your grandmother would like to speak to you. She's a bit tearful, I'm afraid."

There was a sudden silence at the other end of the phone, and a choked breathing.

"Hello, Thomas," came a tearful voice.

"Hello, Grandmother, how are you?" There was a choked sob, and then she continued.

"I'm fine thank you, dear, we're so happy – we can't wait to meet you."

"I can't wait to meet you, either, Grandmother. I must apologise for us not knowing about each other."

Henry's voice came on the line.

"Penny's very overcome, Thomas. We'll have a good chat at the weekend. We'll see you on Friday, my boy."

"Yes, Grandfather, thank you. I'll ring and let you know what time to expect me." They chatted for a few more minutes, then Thomas put down his phone, buried his head in his hands, and tried not to cry.

A few minutes later Thomas looked up – his face hard – and snatched up his mobile phone and began stabbing out a number.

"What are you doing?" asked Sally in alarm.

"Ringing my other grandmother – she owes me an explanation!" Sally's eyes softened as she looked at Thomas. He was so formal. She had always called her grandparents 'Nan' and 'Grandad' like most people – but not Thomas.

"Grandmother, Thomas here. I think you owe me an explanation!"

"What is it, dear?"

"Why didn't you tell me that my father's family were still alive?"

"Oh, you have found Henry and Penny?"

"Yes, and I'm going to meet them this weekend."

"That's lovely, dear, I'm so pleased. Do give them my love."

Thomas was taken aback at Emma's reponse.

"Why wasn't I told?"

"It was your mother's decision, dear. I told her I didn't approve, but she would not listen. As for Penny and Henry, I did let them know. I sent them a Christmas card two years running, with a little note inside telling them about you, but I never heard from them."

"I see," he replied, puzzled.

"Thomas, I think you should know that Penny loved your father very much, and was heartbroken when he died, so go easy on her when you meet."

"Of course I will, and please don't tell my mother I've found them, I don't want her to know."

"My lips are sealed, dear. Now, how did you find them?"

"A girl I've met here, she lives next door to them."

"Well, I'll be blowed!" she exclaimed. "What a coincidence."

"Exactly."

"It was no doubt meant to be. Now, Thomas, you go off to Cropwell and have a lovely weekend."

"Thanks, Grandmother, and goodnight."

"Goodnight, dear." Thomas put his mobile down slowly, on the table, and looked across at Sally's big brown questioning eyes. He repeated his telephone conversation to her. She listened intently.

"What do you think, Sally?"

"I think your mother is a very wicked woman, and she obviously destroyed those Christmas cards your Gran sent to Henry and Penny – because they never arrived – and when you meet them you'll know that's true."

Thomas shook his head, sadly. It was hard to believe that his beautiful mother was so evil.

Henry and Penny were so excited after speaking to Thomas on the phone. Molly and Richard stayed and Henry got out the whisky and sherry and they all sat drinking and talking at once. Penny, between tears of joy was planning the weekend ahead.

"Thomas can have his father's old room, it only wants freshening up," she beamed happily.

Amongst the excitement Henry suddenly remembered their daughter, Amy. He stood up suddenly. "I must ring Amy, she'll be thrilled!" He went out into the hall, where it was quiet, and phoned his daughter. It was Joel who answered the phone.

Amy was sitting on a plush pale green sofa in their beautiful living room facing a glowing fire. The pale green curtains were drawn, shutting out the dark gloomy night. It was a Wednesday, and they were relaxing after dinner.

The phone rang in the hall and Joel went to answer it. He was gone for a while. When he walked slowly back into the room, his forehead was creased below his black and silver hair.

Amy knew there was something wrong as soon as she saw him. "What's wrong, Joel?" she asked. He sat down beside her and took her hand. Her other hand crept up to her hair, which was cut in a short bob, and began to wind strands of it round her fingers.

"That was your father on the phone."

"Is he alright?" she asked anxiously.

"He's very well and happy actually."

"But what's wrong?"

"You're not going to like it, Amy," he swallowed the lump that had risen in his throat.

"Tell me," she begged. Joel looked into her lovely blue eyes.

"When your brother died – his wife was pregnant."

"What!" Amy's face drained of colour. "You can't be serious?"

"I'm afraid so, darling. She had a son, Thomas. He's at Oxford and met Sally Bennett there. She told him about your parents – he'd never been told about them."

"No. Oh, no." whispered Amy, as she began to faint. Joel put an arm round her shoulders and pushed her head down between her knees. She moaned softly. Joel fetched her a brandy, and putting it to her lips made her drink it until the colour came back into her cheeks. She started to cry, her shoulders shaking.

"It's not fair, she wailed, "It's not fair! We've gone all these years taking care not to have children – and Joanna has had a son! It's not fair – and I would have loved a baby!" Joel took his sobbing wife into his arms. She laid her head on his shoulder, and wept into his thick, strong neck, smelling of aftershave. Joel stroked her hair, and laid his cheek against the top of her head.

When her tears had subsided Joel wiped her wet, blotched face with his clean handkerchief.

""What's...what's he like?" she stammered.

"Tall, blond, blue-eyed and apparently very nice, according to Sally."

"We could have had a nice son, if Thomas had one," she whispered, wiping her eyes again.

"Not necessarily, Darling – you made the right decision."

"I don't want to see him."

"Amy, he's coming over on Friday for the weekend, he'll want to see you."

"But Joel, I'm scared."

"Amy, he doesn't know anything – he's an innocent – don't make him suspicious."

"Do you think we should tell Andrew Shaw?" she suddenly asked.

"Yes, I think we should."

"Do you still have those numbers he gave you all those years ago?"

"Yes, I never threw them away, just in case." He got up and searched through his bureau at the far end of the room.

"Here's his home number!" he smiled grimly. "I'll use the mobile." He sat beside Amy on the sofa and rang one of the numbers given to him twenty years ago. He punched out the number of Andrew Shaw and hoped he hadn't moved. Amy clung to Joel's arm as they listened for the phone to ring, but a voice came on the line to say that the code had changed. Joel wrote down the new one and rang again. They waited in suspense.

"Andrew Shaw." They recognised the deep voice with the Scottish lilt.

"Hello, it's Joel Brent here, I don't know if you remember me."

"I do, indeed, Mr. Brent. How are you and Amy?"

"We're fine, thank you."

"What can I do for you, laddie?"

We've had rather a shock this evening – and we thought you should know."

"Go on."

"We've just heard that Amy's brother's wife had a son. He's now about 20 years old, and he's at Oxford."

"Aye, laddie. I heard myself recently. I've been wondering whether to ring you."

"How did you find out?" asked Joel.

"My granddaughter has not long finished at Oxford – she saw him and told me."

"What shall we do?"

"Will you be seeing him?"

"Yes. He's coming to Cropwell this weekend to meet us all.

He didn't know about us until he met the girl who lives next door to Henry – and she told him."

"I see," replied Andrew Shaw slowly. "Mr. Brent, when you have met Thomas, perhaps you would be good enough to ring me, and give me your impression of him."

"Yes, of course," replied Joel.

"Goodnight then, Mr. Brent, and thank you for calling."

"Goodnight." Joel put down the phone. He turned and looked at Amy's sad face, took her in his arms and held her close.

The past had just caught them up.

Thomas and Sally were due at Cropwell shortly after 7 O'clock that Friday night. Henry and Penny had been so excited about his arrival, they had hardly slept. Penny had been cleaning the house, and had gone to town on her son's old room. The house had never looked so clean and tidy. Penny had never been fond of housework, and hated putting things away!

On the Friday morning Henry and Penny had gone to the supermarket to get extra shopping, and Penny then went to the hairdressers to get her hair trimmed and blow-dried. They prepared a tasty supper for when Thomas arrived.

Thomas had been in the same state of excitement as his grandparents, unable to sleep and his inside churning. He could still hardly believe he was going to meet his father's parents – a week ago they had been unknown to him.

Thomas and Sally met up after their lectures on the Friday afternoon. They each went to their flats to finish their packing, and on the way to the station stopped to buy some cigars for Henry and a large bunch of flowers for Penny. Sally had told him not to buy her chocolates as she was always trying to keep her weight down!

Soon Thomas and Sally were sitting on the train heading for Cropwell, after a change at Birmingham New Street. Thomas was feeling nervous and kept rubbing his hands along his thighs. He was wearing an expensive dark brown suit with a cream polo-neck sweater, and had had his hair cut to its normal length. He looked extremely handsome.

He looked across at Sally, who was gazing unseeingly through the dark window of the carriage. He smiled to himself – his mother would have a fit if she could see him with Sally. She was wearing jeans, trainers, and a thick anorak to keep out the cold. She wore no make–up on her pretty face, and her shining curls were windswept. Although Sally wasn't fat, her body was nicely rounded, her shapely legs filled her jeans. She looked across at him and smiled.

"You OK, Thomas?"

"No, I'm scared to death," he replied with a grin. Sally laughed.

"Nobody could be scared of your grandparents – Henry is a dear, and Penny will cry her eyes out – she will be so happy."

Henry and Penny were restless, he smoking a cigar, and she constantly at the window. "I wish we could have picked up them from the station, Henry."

"They insisted they would get a taxi, Pen, we shall just have to wait. And don't forget – not a word about Joanna. We don't want to upset Thomas as soon as he gets here, by criticising his mother."

"Very well, Henry, I promise."

A short while later the front door bell rang – Penny gasped – and a hand went to her throat. Henry stood up and marched into the hall and opened the front door, to see his grandson, standing before him, tall, and handsome, an overnight bag in one hand, and a bunch of flowers in the other.

"Grandfather?"

"Thomas? Good to see you, my boy, come along in." Henry led Thomas into the hall. "Dump your bag anywhere, Thomas," smiled

Henry. Thomas dropped his bag on the hall floor, the smell of jacket potatoes cooking in the oven wafted in from the kitchen and made him feel hungry.

Thomas and Henry looked at each other and shook hands and smiled broadly. Henry was a little shorter than Thomas, with thin grey hair, an aquiline face, and warm blue eyes behind horn-rimmed glasses. Thomas liked him instantly. Suddenly there was a cry, and Thomas turned to see a small, plump lady with soft permed grey hair, staring at him with large hazel eyes filled with tears. "Oh, Thomas!" she gasped, and promptly burst into tears.

Thomas put his free arm round his sweet little grandmother, and she buried her face in his sweater. He hugged her, and guided by Henry led into the living room, which he noticed was cosy and comfortable if a little worn. The brown and gold carpet looked clean, but old, as did the long gold velvet curtains covering the windows, and the brown leather suite had seen better days. There was a coffee table in front of the settee laden with newspapers and a large ash–tray. Opposite was a glowing gas fire, a TV and another small table by the fire, with two beautiful wedding photos and a vase of flowers. One of the photos was of Amy and Joel, and the other was one of his parents – the same photo his mother had at home. There could be no mistake – these people really were his grandparents – they were not a dream!

Thomas led Penny to the settee and sat down beside her, laying his flowers on the coffee table, he fumbled in his pocket for a handkerchief and wiped her eyes.

"Thank you, Thomas. I'm sorry to make such a fool of myself, but you look so like your father. It's all been such a shock," she babbled. "Now, let me look at you."

Thomas and Penny looked at each other and smiled.

"Hello, Grandmother."

"Hello, Thomas." They both suddenly laughed and hugged each other.

Henry sat in his armchair, and then they were all talking at once. Henry's lined face was alight and Penny's was glowing with happiness. Her eyes were shining with joy, and her small hands constantly touching Thomas's sleeve. Thomas had chuckled to himself when he had taken off his jacket and Penny had told him to 'dump it anywhere'.

Thomas did not mention his mother, but did pass on the greetings from Emma, and told Henry and Penny about the Christmas cards she had sent. They looked at each other and frowned.

"We never heard from them at all," said Penny puzzled. "I sent them a Christmas card for a couple of years, too. They must have got lost in the post. Never mind, Thomas, you can give our love to Emma and Marcus. We were always very fond of Emma, and she was so kind to me at your father's funeral," she added sadly.

The smell of jacket potatoes was getting stronger. "Goodness, the supper!" cried Penny.

"I'll see to it, Penny, you look after Thomas," smiled Henry. He picked up the flowers from the coffee table and took them into the kitchen. Whilst Penny and Thomas were chatting, Henry got three steaks out of the fridge and put them under the grill. A bowl of salad and a plate of crusty bread and butter were already prepared and covered in cling–film. Three trays were laid with plates and cutlery. Henry opened a bottle of wine, and took it into the living room with three glasses, along with salt, pepper and a jar of mustard.

"You'll find us very informal here, Thomas," said Henry cheerfully," are you alright with a tray on your lap?"

"That's fine Grandfather, I'd rather be informal."

"Good lad!" rejoined Henry.

Soon all three of them were tucking into a tasty supper. Thomas was hungry and ate every bit, followed by cheese and biscuits and coffee. He felt relaxed and happy with this friendly easy–going couple. When they had finished eating Henry cleared away the plates, and they sat drinking wine and chatting, trying to catch up with a lost twenty years.

During the evening Penny showed Thomas many family photos, including those of Amy and his father when they were children. Thomas was fascinated by them all. Some of the more recent ones included an elderly woman with Henry. They were both smiling and happy.

“That was Henry’s sister,” pointed out Penny. A knot formed in Thomas’s stomach as he remembered Sally’s story.

“Sister?” he asked.

“Oh, yes,” cried Penny. “Do tell Thomas about her, Henry.”

Henry paused and lit a cigar. “Well,” he began, “it was really quite amazing. It all happened when Amy was on her honeymoon. It was a Sunday morning and I was out in the back garden mowing the lawn, when the phone rang. It was an American woman on the phone and she asked me if I was born on 1st March, 1942, and when I said that I was, she said that I was her long lost baby brother and could she come and see me. She was on holiday in England on her own, as her husband had died, and she had no children. She arrived here later that day. She told me her name was Fransiska Jeffries, and that she had been brought up in America, and it was only when her parents were dying, that she was told the truth about her past.

Apparently our mother and father were born and bred in Berlin in Germany. Our father had been a soldier. His name was Heinrich Koner and our mother, Christina. Well, Fransiska was born first and I followed a few years later. I was called Heinrich, after our father, who died before I was born. Whilst I was still a baby my mother was sent on a mission of some kind to England, and took me with her, leaving Fransiska behind with our aunt Lilli and her husband. Lilli being my mother’s sister. Not long afterwards Lilli and her husband were killed in a bombing raid, leaving Fransiska alone. Friends of the family found her. They didn’t know exactly where my mother was, except it was somewhere in the Midlands. They knew that Lilli had sent her a message to say that they were going to America and my mother was to meet them there. So, this couple smuggled Fransiska out of Germany and took her to America to an arranged address. My mother never turned up, so they brought her up as their own child.”

“That’s amazing!” cried Thomas, “but how did she find you?”

Henry waved a finger in the air. “Simple really, Thomas. She was told that our mother had changed her name to Caroline Kendal, and mine to Henry. She realised that our mother could be dead or remarried so she decided to look for me. She simply came to England, and starting in the Midlands she went through all the telephone directories ringing up every H. Kendal until she got me – right name and date of birth.”

"But how could you be certain that you were the right brother?" asked Thomas frowning. Henry smiled.

"When you meet Amy, and you look at that photo – you will see the likeness. Also, Thomas, my mother's past was always a bit of a mystery. I remember Amy trying to trace my ancestors after she moved into my mother's cottage, and she never could find anything."

"Were you never curious about your past, Grandfather?"

"I was, Thomas, but I thought that if my ancestors were German soldiers, it might be best to just let sleeping dogs lie – so that is what I did."

"Fransiska was lovely, so like Amy," added Penny. "We were so sorry when she died a few years ago. I can remember when Amy came back from her honeymoon and we told her. She fainted with shock."

"And you thought she was pregnant!" added Henry, pointing his cigar at her.

"I know. I was so disappointed – and she never has been pregnant," she said sadly.

"I wonder why your mother came over here when there was a war on?"

"I've no idea, Thomas, it's always been a mystery," replied Henry, shaking his head.

Thomas sat for a moment – he was sure that Henry's mother had something to do with the mystery surrounding his father, but he remained silent.

The three of them talked late into the night, getting to know each other. When they were finally ready to go to bed, Thomas gave Henry the box of cigars, which he accepted with pleasure, and Penny took him up to his room.

"Thomas, I've given you your father's old room. It will now be your room, and you can come and visit us whenever you like."

"If you want anything of your father's just take it." She let Thomas into the room and turned on the light. She turned and looked up at him, and he bent his head and kissed her on the cheek.

"Thank you, Grandmother, and goodnight."

"Goodnight, dear," Penny whispered, and left the room. She touched her cheek where he had kissed her. "Thank you, God," she whispered to herself, "for giving me this wonderful grandson."

Thomas looked round his father's old room. It smelled of furniture polish and air freshener. He smiled to himself knowing that his sweet little grandmother had spent her time cleaning up the room and making it nice for him. The room was not very big. The walls were plain magnolia, the carpet blue, and the curtains and bed linen were a blue and green pattern. The bed was behind the door, and opposite was a fitted unit of wardrobes and a dressing table in light wood. On the walls were shelves of books and photos of his father – some when he was young and some of when he was older, including one large one of him in his cap and gown.

Thomas dumped his bag on the bed and went over to the books, picking one at random. Inside, written in childish handwriting was –

'To Thomas, happy birthday, love Amy, xxx'

He picked up a larger one – the biography of a famous cricketer. Inside was written, 'To Thomas, happy Christmas, all our love, Mum and Dad.' Thomas was deeply touched. He replaced the book as he saw a cricket bat lying against the wall. He picked it up and stroked the smooth wood. His father's cricket bat – the father he never knew. Thomas walked round the bedroom, touching all the things that had been his father's. There was nothing like this at Westlake Manor, as his father had never lived there. Thomas felt close to his father for the first time in his life. He went to the window and drew the curtains, his face grim. His mother had tried to deny him all this – it was unforgivable!

When Thomas finally got into bed he found it hard to sleep. He thought about his two grandmothers sending each other those Christmas cards, and then not bothering to contact each other. Why on earth didn't one of them just pick up a phone?

He heard Henry and Penny go to the bathroom and then to their bedroom. The house became silent. He lay there thinking about the day's events and of the lovely couple who had welcomed him to his father's home.

The following morning Thomas woke to the delicious smell of frying bacon. He got up hastily, washed and dressed and ran downstairs to the kitchen. He entered to find Henry sitting at the table reading the morning paper, and Penny standing by the cooker making breakfast. They both looked up at him and smiled.

"Good morning, Thomas, did you sleep well, dear?" asked Penny brightly.

"Very well, thank you," he replied smiling.

"Coffee's on the table, help yourself, Thomas," urged Henry. Thomas sat down beside his grandfather and they started chatting. They were all soon enjoying a tasty breakfast together.

After breakfast Henry and Penny took Thomas out and showed him round Cropwell. He saw the schools his father had gone to as a boy, and the schools where Henry had been a teacher.

At lunchtime they stopped at one of Cropwell's old pubs for lunch, where they enjoyed a ploughman's lunch and a glass of cider. After lunch they returned home where Henry and Thomas relaxed and watched the football on the TV and Penny went upstairs for a rest.

"We'll be having a late night tonight, Thomas," explained Henry. "We're going to Bishops Fell with Sally and her parents. You'll be meeting Amy and Joel, and we are all going to the King's Head for a meal."

"Sounds great," replied Thomas, who was looking forward to meeting his only aunt for the first time.

Henry and Thomas enjoyed their football match, and when Penny got up she made a pot of tea, and sliced up some cake. They all sat chatting until it was time to get ready for their evening out.

By 7.30 they were all ready. Henry and Thomas were smartly dressed in suits – Henry in a formal one and Thomas in an expensive, trendy one with a silky sweater. Penny was wearing a new dress, and kept patting her hair.

"Here they are!" she cried, as Sally and her parents knocked the door. Penny went off to let them in and they all walked into the living room. Thomas was introduced to Molly and Richard – they were older that he had expected. Their only daughter, Sally, must have been born fairly late in their lives.

"Nice to meet you, Thomas," greeted Richard cheerfully, who was tall and thin with straight fair hair.

"Thomas, hello. You do look like your father," smiled Molly. She was short and slim with brown, curly hair, like Sally.

Sally – Thomas stared at her in amazement. She looked stunning in a long black silky dress and long black jacket. Her freshly washed brown curls were soft and shining, tendrils of hair gently touching her beautifully made up face, with sparkling green eyeshadow enhancing her lovely big brown eyes, and frosted peach lipstick showing up her wide smiling mouth. Gold earrings glinted through her hair, and she looked tall and graceful in high–heeled black shoes.

"Sally, you look fantastic!" gasped Thomas.

"About time, too," interrupted her father, "she looks like a scarecrow most of the time!"

"Thanks Dad," grinned Sally. She looked at Thomas. "I warn you – at the stroke of midnight I turn into a witch!" Everyone laughed, and Thomas could feel his spirits rise – he was looking forward to the evening.

"The taxi's here, come on everyone!" cried Henry. They all made their way outside and got into a "Super" taxi that comfortably held six people. It was arranged that Sally and her parents would be dropped off at The Kings Head, whilst Henry and Penny would take Thomas to Jade Cottage to meet Amy and Joel, and they would walk back to the pub together.

Henry, Penny and Thomas walked up the path to the cottage, which was built of grey stone, with mullioned windows. A faint light shone through the curtains. The door was at the side of the cottage, and they had to pass Joel's sleek, black car parked under the carport.

Henry rang the bell and the door was opened by Joel. Thomas recognised him from the wedding photo given to him by Sally, but he was now more heavily built and his black hair was streaked with silver.

"Hello, there," smiled Joel, "you must be Thomas." The two men shook hands. "Nice to meet you."

"Nice to meet you, too, Joel."

Thomas was led through a stone-flagged passage and into a cosy living room with a low ceiling, heavy oak beams and a glowing gas fire, that looked real with flames dancing over coals. The room was delicately furnished in peaches and cream with touches of green. He was introduced to Amy, his father's sister. She looked a little older and thinner than in her wedding photo. Her hair was now shorter with strands of white, cut in a bob touching her chin. She was dressed in a long silky cream dress and dark brown velvet jacket. Thomas held out his hand to her, but his stomach flipped over when he saw the naked fear in her big blue eyes.

"Hello, Aunt Amy, it's lovely to meet you," he said shyly.

"H...hello, Thomas. You have given us a big surprise." He smiled, and leaning forward he kissed her cheek. A blush crept into her face, and she was rescued by her husband, who went up and put an arm round her shoulders.

"Your cottage is beautiful," continued Thomas, trying to quell the knot in his stomach.

"Thank you, Ill show you round the next time you are here."

Right," said Henry, "are we ready?" Joel switched off the fire and turned out the lights as they all moved out of the cottage, and walked along the village street to the Kings Head.

"She's frightened of me," thought Thomas. "She knows something about me that the others don't, I'm positive."

Within minutes they were inside the pub. Everyone was soon chatting and laughing, and drinks were being handed round. The Kings Head was spacious, although it was very old, like many old pubs it had the low ceilings and heavy beams. Velvet curtains were drawn over the mullioned windows, and brasses and pictures of horses and huntsmen decorated the walls. There was a huge fireplace in the centre with a lounge on one side and the restaurant on the other.

Henry made it clear that the meal and drinks were his treat, and everyone was to have whatever they wanted. A table was set for them at the far end, and a champagne bucket was placed at the head of the table. The Kendals were well known in the Kings Head, and Thomas found himself meeting and shaking hands with staff and customers, who were all amazed to see him.

When it was time to order they all sat down. Henry sat at the head of the table with Thomas, Sally and Molly on his left, and Penny, Amy and Joel on his right, and Richard at the bottom.

Bottles of wine were soon placed on the table, and champagne in the bucket, and meals were ordered.

They all had a wonderful evening, everyone wanting to speak to Thomas at once. He was overwhelmed with the affection everyone was bestowing upon him. Amy became friendlier after a few drinks, but he could see the anxiety in her eyes, and saw her hand shake every time she lit a cigarette. What was wrong?

Thomas kept gazing at Sally, who looked so glamorous.

"How's it going?" she whispered.

"Marvellous!" he replied.

They stayed at the pub until one a.m. There were still many customers having a late night. By the time their taxi arrived Penny was tiddly and Henry had to help her up out of her chair! They said goodnight to Amy and Joel, and Thomas kissed her, saying, "see you tomorrow." His aunt and Joel were coming to Henry's for their Sunday lunch.

The taxi eventually drove the Kendals and the Bennetts back to Cropwell, and Amy and Joel walked the short distance home to the cottage. It was cold, dark and misty.

"Are you alright, Amy?"

"Yes, thanks."

"What did you think of him?"

"He seems very sweet."

"Is he anything like your brother?"

"He looks like him, but he is different."

"How?"

"Well, my brother was outgoing and confident, and he was always watching people, as if he was weighing them up. Thomas seems more...soft and gentle and kind."

"I liked him – he seems an extremely nice young man, and very well–mannered."

"Yes. I got the feeling that he cares more about Mum and Dad, than my brother ever did, and he's only just met them."

"I still can't believe that your brother's wife never told Thomas about your parents and you."

"Joanna never did like us. She thought we weren't good enough for her."

Amy and Joel reached the cottage, let themselves in and went straight to bed. Amy's thoughts were in turmoil. It was a long time before she slept.

The Kendals slept late on Sunday morning, and Thomas woke once more to the smell of frying bacon. By the time he had showered and dressed and reached the kitchen, breakfast was almost ready.

"Good morning, dear," smiled Penny.

"Morning, Thomas, help yourself to coffee," said Henry, cheerful as always.

"Are you feeling alright, Grandmother?" asked Thomas.

"You mean is she sober?" teased Henry.

"Something like that," replied Thomas with a sheepish grin. He sat at the table and poured himself a coffee.

Thomas found himself smiling. What a contrast there was between his two grandmothers! Emma, who had never cooked a meal in her life, and dressed like a fashion model from morning til night – and Penny, standing over a hot stove, her grey hair tousled, dressed in a faded blue woollen dressing gown, with a slip of nightie peeping beneath the hem, and an old pair of blue slippers on her small feet.

Penny brought their breakfast to the kitchen table – bacon, eggs and tomatoes, a plate of hot toast, a dish of butter and a pot of marmalade. Thomas tucked into his breakfast, thinking how nice it would be to have one put before him every day of the week!

After breakfast Penny shooed the two men out of the kitchen, whilst she cleared up and went to get dressed. Thomas and Henry sat in the living room chatting quietly.

Later in the morning Henry took Thomas for a walk before going to the local pub for a drink before dinner.

"I'll send Joel down to meet you when he gets here, and Amy can help me with the dinner," said Penny as they left the house.

Henry and Thomas left the warmth of the house to face a cold but sunny morning. They turned left and walked down the Cropwell Road and turned left again down a small street and headed for the woods. As they reached the entrance to the woods they were met by falling autumn leaves, and faced a long pathway – a carpet of red and gold stretching before them.

They walked slowly through the carpet of leaves, listening to birds chirruping and the rustle of small animals that had not yet hibernated.

Henry and Thomas talked animatedly to each other. They found that they had a lot in common, and had the same ideas about many subjects. Every now and again they passed people walking their dogs. They stopped and spoke to Henry as their dogs snuffled and scampered through the dead leaves.

"Do you know everyone?" asked Thomas in surprise.

"Pretty well," replied Henry.

"I'd like to be a teacher," stated Thomas, "I don't want to go into politics."

"Well, it's a good profession, and very rewarding, Thomas."

"What would I have to do?"

"Finish your law degree – it would be a waste to drop out now. You would then need to go to another university and take a teaching course – you could not get a teaching job in a state school without teaching qualifications – you could study for a B.A. or a BSc. – it would take three or four years."

"Will you help me?"

"Of course, Thomas, no problem."

Thomas felt a warm glow in his heart. He liked Henry – he felt he could discuss anything with him – he was so easy to talk to.

"I'm sorry my mother never told you about me," stammered Thomas. "It was unforgivable of her, and I feel dreadful." Henry patted his arm.

"Don't worry, Thomas, it's not your fault – and don't be too hard on your mother. I assume she has been a good mother to you – and we all have our faults."

"Thanks, Grandfather, you're very understanding," replied Thomas gratefully – although he had no intention of forgiving his mother. Henry continued.

"When you have been a teacher for many years, Thomas, you get to know and understand people – eventually nothing that people do will come as a surprise."

Thomas wanted to confide in Henry and told him about the row he had had with his mother. "Is it true?" he asked frowning.

"I'm afraid so, Thomas," said Henry quietly. "I know he hated black people and crippled people, and had no time for anyone who wouldn't work or took drugs."

"So, he did lie?" said Thomas flatly.

"He wouldn't have lasted five minutes as an M.P. if he hadn't"

"Yes, I suppose that's true."

"Has this upset you?"

"It's been a shock. It seems that my idol had feet of clay."

"That's life, Thomas."

"I don't want to be like that."

"You're not, Thomas. Just stay as you are – and by the way, don't mention this to Penny, it would upset her. She thought your father was perfect."

"So did I," thought Thomas, sadly.

They reached the end of the woodland path, turned left, walked along the side of the railway line and turned left again, bringing them to the other end of the Cropwell Road. Within minutes they were in the pub, the "Fox and Hounds." The pub was a smaller version of the Kings Head in Bishops Fell, with its grey stone walls and oak beams. They walked into the lounge and found a table by the window, near the fire. Thomas went up to the bar and got them both a lager. Henry lit a cigar and they sat and waited for Joel. The pub was busy – most people sitting at tables and a crowd standing at the bar. The room was filled with low chatter and a haze of smoke drifted over their heads.

Thomas looked up to see Joel threading his way through the lounge. He smiled as he greeted them. "You two ready for another pint?" They nodded and Joel brought three pints over to their table. "Dinner's at 2.30." he reminded them.

By the time the men got home dinner was ready. The dining room, which looked out onto the back garden, was laid, and Penny and Amy were bringing in dishes if food. There was a plate full of sliced turkey and stuffing, a large dish of roast and creamed potatoes, a dish of Yorkshire puddings, and bowls of vegetables – sprouts, carrots and peas, plus a large jug of gravy.

"That looks good!" exclaimed Henry, rubbing his hands together. He poured everyone a glass of wine. They all enjoyed their meal. After dinner Penny and Amy cleared away and brought in a large lemon meringue pie and a jug of cream. Thomas tucked in happily – he loved Penny's cooking. When he had finished, he looked at Penny and smiled.

"That was delicious!" She beamed at him happily.

After the table was cleared they all moved into the conservatory, which was warm in the afternoon sun. They sat drinking coffee, chatting and relaxed – the washing up left in the kitchen – the door shut.

By six o'clock it was time for Thomas to leave. Sally had come round with her father, who was going to take them to the station.

Thomas kissed Penny and Amy, and shook hands with Henry and Joel. "Thank you for a wonderful weekend – all of you."

Penny hugged him. "It's been wonderful for us, too, Thomas – please do come and see is whenever you wish – you'll always be welcome."

"Thank you, I will."

The Kendal family stood in the doorway as Thomas and Sally left and waved goodbye. Penny's eyes were shimmering with tears of happiness.

Thomas and Sally were now on the train that was snaking its way through dark fields. The train was nearly empty but would be full by the time they arrived in Birmingham.

They sat opposite each other. She sat looking at him, her eyes shining, her hands tucked between her knees.

"Well, what do you think of your father's family now you have met them?"

"Great!"

"Penny?"

"She's adorable, so sweet and motherly."

"And Henry?"

"He's just like you said – kind and gentle and intelligent – he's so understanding and made me feel good inside."

"I knew he would. And Amy?"

Thomas frowned.

"What's wrong, Thomas?"

"She's scared of me."

"What! Don't be silly."

"She is, Sally. I saw the fear in her eyes when we met. Joel knows too, he was protecting her."

"But why?"

"I don't know," he said, slowly, "but I think that Amy and Joel know something about my father that Henry and Penny don't."

"I can't think of anything."

"Sally, don't you think it's rather odd that Andrew Shaw should be so afraid that I had been born, and then Amy should be so scared of me? There's got to be something."

"But, Thomas there's no way that Amy could possibly have known Andrew Shaw. He was the head of Special Branch in London – there's no way they could have met!"

"They could both know something about my father separately."

"Yes, of course, you're right."

"Sally, I don't want Amy to be afraid of me."

"Why don't you send her some flowers? I can give you her address in Melton Mowbray."

"Thanks, Sally, I will. That's a good idea."

Two days later Amy was at home, when a large basket of flowers was delivered to her door. When she opened the small envelope to see who it was from, she found a card which read:

'To Amy, the only aunt I have in the whole world. Love Thomas.'

Two large tears rolled down Amy's face. One a tear of happiness for Thomas' lovely gift, the other a tear of sadness for the child she had never had.

Thomas and Sally made a couple more visits to Cropwell, and Thomas agreed to stay with Henry and Penny for Christmas and New Year. They were thrilled.

Joanna was furious. Thomas told her he was staying with friends, but she had planned a skiing holiday in Austria for them both.

Thomas told her to go on her own.

She did.

CHAPTER SIX

FELICITY - 2011 - 2012

When Fliss left Oxford she was sad at leaving Thomas, but looking forward to her new life travelling all over the world. She was going to visit each country where her father had tours, and work with each tour guide so that she would get to know them all and their routines. When she had done this she would be able to fill in anywhere she was needed.

Before leaving, Fliss went to visit her grandparents. She was not looking forward to talking about Thomas to her grandfather.

When she arrived at their house she was greeted by the dog, who jumped up to her, his tail wagging, his tongue flapping out of his mouth. Fliss patted him and he barked happily.

"Hello, dear," smiled her grandmother, "would you like a cup of tea?"

"Yes, please, Gran. Where's Gramps?"

"In the living room, dear."

Fliss walked into the living room to see her grandfather sitting in the chair, looking rather pale.

"Gramps, are you alright?" she asked, her green eyes anxious. Andrew Shaw rubbed a hand over his chest.

"I'm fine, lassie," he lied.

"No, you're not," she argued.

"Well, ticker's a bit dicky, that's all," he replied with a grin.

"You must take care of yourself," she ordered firmly.

"You ready for the off?" he asked.

"Yes," she replied happily. "I'm off tomorrow morning – flying to Spain first. I'm doing Europe, The Canaries, America and Mexico, too, isn't it wonderful?"

Rather you than me, lassie."

Fliss's grandmother came in carrying a tray of tea and biscuits. She poured them all a drink, and Andrew asked her if she had any more news about Thomas Kendal. Her stomach turned over.

"Nothing more, Gramps – he's just a nice guy. Can't you give me a clue? I might be able to help you more."

"No, Fliss, it's highly confidential – I cannot tell you."

Fliss was still puzzled, but knew she would get nothing more out of him.

Fliss finally said goodbye to her grandparents, and set off home to finish her packing.

The next morning Fliss flew off to Spain. She knew she was going to have a busy life, working all hours – meeting flights coming in and taking tourists back to the airport for flights out. There would be sight-seeing tours to organise and times when she would have to be at each hotel to deal with guests, hand out information and sort out problems.

There would be many long flights to cope with, especially when she would suddenly have a last minute trip to America or Mexico to help a tour guide who had become short-staffed or needed help. Fliss would often be very tired, and was warned that her 'body–clock' would go 'haywire'.

In the November of that year, whilst Thomas was meeting his new family in Cropwell, Fliss was in Lanzarote. The weather was very hot, and Fliss and Sue, the tour guide she was working with, had just taken a tour round the miles of volcanic hills, ending up with a stop at Fire Mountain, to see the amazing affects of the hot volcano. The tourist had stood fascinated as water was poured into a fissure, and seconds later saw it shoot into the air as hot steam. This had been followed by a bundle of hay being pushed into another fissure on the end of a pitchfork, only to come out covered in flames. The tourists had then been taken up to the circular restaurant at the top of Fire Mountain to see a massive grille resting on top of a large, deep hole – the heat from the volcano cooking the sizzling meat lying on top of the grille.

Fliss was glad when the coach got back to the hotel, as she didn't feel well. She looked at Sue, a tall, sun-tanned girl with short, blonde hair and pale blue eyes.

"Sue, I feel awful."

"What's up, Fliss?"

"I just feel dreadful."

"Come on, I'll take you back to the flat." Sue put an arm round Fliss's waist, and they walked slowly to their flat. Sue unlocked the door, and as Fliss staggered to her bedroom, she fainted. Sue rushed over to her. As Fliss came round Sue took off her shoes and helped her onto the bed.

"I'll get you some water," she said softly, and dashed off to the kitchen and got a bottle of water from the fridge and a glass from the cupboard. She went back to the bedroom, poured some water into the glass, and gave it to Fliss, who took a few sips.

"Thanks, Sue." Fliss put the glass down on the bedside table, and lay back against the pillows.

"How do you feel now?"

"A bit better, thanks. I just felt sick and faint. It must be the heat." Sue suddenly laughed.

"You're not pregnant are you, Fliss?" Fliss lay very still.

"Fliss?"

"Yes."

"You OK?"

"I don't know." Sue frowned.

"I was only joking."

"I know...but..." Fliss remembered her night with Thomas. "Oh, shit!"

"You *are* pregnant, aren't you?"

"I...I'm...not sure..."

"When was your last period?"

"I can't remember."

"Can't remember! Fliss you must be mad!"

"I've been so busy, I just hadn't noticed. I've not had morning sickness, and I've not put on any weight," she added

"But you could be pregnant?"

"Yes," whispered Fliss, horrified. "I could be."

"When did it happen?"

"My last night at Oxford. I've not slept with anyone since then."

"But, Fliss, that's four months ago!"

"I know."

"You idiot, why aren't you on the pill?"

"There's a history of thrombosis in my family, my doctor said I shouldn't take it...it's the red hair, you know." she grinned weakly.

"Well, why didn't you take a 'morning after' pill?"

"I just didn't get round to it."

"Fliss, I cannot believe you could be so careless!"

"Neither can I," replied Fliss wiping a hand across her brow. Sue stood up.

"I'm going to the Farmacia to get you a pregnancy testing kit – and don't argue!"

"OK. Thanks, Sue." Sue left the room, grabbed her handbag, and dashed off to the chemist. Fliss heard the door slam as her friend went out. She lay back and closed her eyes. If she was pregnant, she was having Thomas Kendal's child. God – what a mess! She was too far gone to have a termination. What on earth would her parents say? And Gramps? – he would be horrified – she would never be able to tell anyone who the father was.

She turned her head to one side, and looked at KAT, sitting primly on the bedside cabinet. "It's all your fault," she whispered.

Sue was soon back. She hurried into the bedroom with a small box in a bag.

"Here you are. It's dead easy. You do a wee in this little dish – dip in one of these 'thingies' and if it turns red, you're pregnant!"

Fliss eased herself off the bed, and taking the box, made her way unhappily to the bathroom. She came out a few minutes later, her face crumpled.

"Oh, Fliss," Sue took her friend in her arms as Fliss started to cry.

"What are you going to do, Fliss?"

"I'll have to go home – soon anyway – I'll have to see a doctor."

“Who’s the father, Fliss?”

“Don’t even ask!”

“Is he married?”

“No.”

“Are you going to tell him?”

“No.”

“Why not?”

“There’s no point – and I don’t want him to know.”

“OK.”

Fliss lay on her bed in a state of shock – her mind in a whirl.

Two weeks later Fliss was due for some leave. She flew back to England and landed at Gatwick after a three and a half-hour flight. After collecting her luggage she made her way to the railway station, where she caught a local train to Barnet, to her parent’s home. Her parents, Edward and Jill made a big fuss of her.

“We have missed you, Fliss,” smiled her mother, giving her a big hug.

“I’ve missed you both, too.”

“Been working hard I hope!” teased her father.

“Of course,” she replied, trying to keep the unease out of her voice.

After dinner Fliss told her parents she was tired, and thankfully escaped to her room.

The following morning, after breakfast, whilst her parents were out, Fliss went off to see her doctor. She sat in the waiting room, twiddling her fingers nervously, her inside turning over.

When she finally got in to see her doctor, she was soon examined and her pregnancy confirmed. She was given a date in April, and sent to the hospital for a medical check up and a scan.

Fliss drove to the hospital slowly – her hands gripping the steering wheel – her legs trembling – her face pale. She parked her car and made her way to the Maternity Unit. She went to the Reception Desk to check in, and was told to wait.

She sat in a stunned silence, looking at all the pictures on the walls of bouncing babies, and adverts for milk and babies injections. She looked round at the other patients, some of them heavily pregnant, chatting to each other. She suddenly felt very lonely.

Eventually a pretty dark-haired nurse called her name, and she was taken into a surgery. The nurse took all her details, her blood pressure, and her weight. The nurse chatted kindly to her, putting her at her ease. Fliss soon found herself lying on a bed, a black disc moving over her abdomen. She looked at the TV screen and gazed in amazement as she saw the baby inside her.

"Your baby is small. Do you want to know the sex?"

"No...no...thank you." stammered Fliss. When the scan was over, the nurse gave her a black and white picture of the baby, which she had taken from the machine. She then gave Fliss an appointment for four weeks time.

When Fliss got home she saw her mother's car parked on the drive, outside their large ivy–clad house. She locked her car and slowly went into the house, to find her mother in the kitchen. As she walked in her mother looked up.

"What's wrong, Fliss?" asked Jill Shaw, as she saw her daughter's distraught face.

"Mum...I...I'm... pregnant."

"Oh, Fliss!" Her mother went up to Fliss, and put her arms round her daughter, whose lovely freckled face was now wet with tears. Jill took her daughter into the lounge, and they sat down on the settee together.

"Now," smiled Jill, "what are all those tears for?"

"I'm sorry, Mum, but it's been a bit of a shock."

"Never mind, dear, these things happen – now how far gone are you?"

"Four and a half months."

"Four and a half months! Good gracious, Fliss, your pregnancy is half over already."

"I know."

"Who's the father?"

"Someone I met at Oxford."

"Are you going to tell him?"

"No, I don't want him to know."

"But what if he finds out?"

"He won't – he lives a long way from here."

"But, darling, he had a right to know, and he may want to pay maintenance."

"No, Mum, please..."

"Alright, Fliss. Now, how are you feeling?"

"I'm...OK I haven't had any symptoms, or put on any weight. Oh, I've got a picture here." She took the photo out of her bag and showed it to her mother.

"Of, Fliss, just look, my first grandchild!" her mother beamed.

"You're not angry, Mum?"

"Of course not, darling."

"What about Dad? What will he say about my career?"

"Leave your father to me. Now can I make a suggestion?"

"Go on, Mum."

"Well, if you want to go on working after the baby is born – you could do some short trips, and I'll look after the baby whilst you are away."

"Oh, Mum, would you?"

"Of course, I'd love to, but I would insist that you only do short trips, as you must spend some time with your baby, so that he or she will know that you are its mother." Fliss brightened up, and hugged her mother.

Soon the two women were chatting about the baby, and all the things they would to have to buy and do. Fliss was greatly relieved by her mother's attitude, and amused at her excitement at becoming a grandmother.

"What about names, Fliss?"

"Well, if I have a boy with red hair, which means he will probably have my green eyes, I shall call him Andrew after Gramps. If I have a girl with my colouring, I shall call her Jade. Otherwise I don't know."

The rest of the day was spent on baby talk. Fliss's father was going to be late home, and she left it to her mother to give him the news.

As Fliss lay on her back in bed that night, she suddenly felt the first delicate kicks of her tiny unborn baby.

In April, the following year, Fliss gave birth to a baby daughter. She weighed in at just 2.438 kilograms (5lb 6oz), and was named Jade Shaw.

When Jade's birth was registered her certificate stated – 'father – unknown'.

CHAPTER SEVEN

TROUBLE – 2012

When Joanna got back from her winter ski–ing holiday, she was still angry with Thomas for not going with her. She was furious because she did not know where he was or who he was with. He certainly was not growing up the way she had expected. He was nothing like his father at all. Her son was soft and weak and sentimental like her in–laws, she hoped to God that he never met them – that meek and mild unambitious Henry, and that silly stupid Penny. With a bit of luck they were dead and gone.

Joanna's mind was working fast. The only way she would be able to find out what Thomas was doing, was to have him followed. Without telling her parents she contacted an old colleague, who put her on to a very good private detective called Abercrombie. She contacted him and asked him to keep her son under surveillance, and send her regular reports. She told the detective that she was worried in case Thomas was kidnapped, and wanted him protected.

Thomas, in the meantime, was growing very fond of his new grandparents, and made every effort to visit them regularly. He and Sally had become good friends, as she would sometimes go with him, and visit her parents. Sally was often tied up at weekends. She had a lovely singing voice, and was now a member of the university choir, and they often had meetings of some description at weekends.

Thomas was frustrated at having to go down to Cropwell on the train, and decided that on his next visit home he would collect his car. He would have to leave it at the Park and Ride car park, but it couldn't be helped.

Thomas was reluctant to go home, but towards the end of February it was Emma's birthday, which gave him an excuse to go to Westlake Manor and collect the car.

The Saturday of Emma's birthday, Burrows drove down to Keble to pick up Thomas. He would arrive at Westlake Manor at lunchtime, and stay until Sunday afternoon.

"Good morning, Burrows, and how are you?" asked Thomas, as he walked up to the limousine.

"Fine, thank you, young Thomas – and you?"

"Very well, thanks."

Thomas settled himself in the back of the car, his overnight bag beside him on the seat.

"Have you been looking after my car?" asked Thomas politely.

"I certainly have, Thomas. She's running beautifully."

"Good. Is she full of petrol?"

"Yes."

"That's good. I shall be taking my car back with me."

"Miss Joanna won't like that," replied Burrows cautiously.

"Tough!" replied Thomas, his eyes hard. Burrows remained silent, frowning. This wasn't the Thomas he knew.

When Thomas finally arrived at Westlake Manor, his grandparents greeted him.

"Thomas, dear, how lovely to see you. Do come in out of the cold – it's freezing out there today."

"Hello, Grandmother, happy birthday!" he smiled, handing her a birthday card and a present – a box of her favourite, very expensive chocolates.

"Thank you, dear, you are so thoughtful."

"Hello, Grandfather."

"Thomas, it's good to see you," Marcus patted him affectionately on the shoulder.

"Where's mother?" asked Thomas quietly.

"In the drawing room, dear. She doesn't look too happy," she warned.

Thomas walked into the drawing room, after taking a deep breath. As he walked in his wary eyes met his mother's cold, icy ones. As usual Joanna was groomed to perfection, her golden hair softly touching the shoulders of her dark blue dress.

"Hello, Mother."

"Hello!" she stormed. "Where have you been these last few months?"

"Busy."

"You are a liar, Thomas!"

"What is that supposed to mean?"

"It means that you have been sneaking down to Cropwell, and visiting the Kendals!" Thomas was appalled.

"How did you know?" he snapped.

"How did I know?" she screamed, her eyes blazing. "I've had you followed of course! I know everything you have been up to. I know about this dreadful, scruffy girl who lives next door to Henry and Penny. And I know about your friends, the black one and that dreadful boy with the ponytail." Thomas was livid.

"You've what! You've had me followed," yelled Thomas, his face white, his fists clenched. "How dare you have me followed about, and how dare you insult my friends!"

"And how dare you speak to me like that – I am your mother!"

"Mother...Mother!..How can you call yourself a mother, when you have lied to me all my life! You told me my father's parents were dead! You've denied Henry and Penny their only grandson for twenty years – it's unforgivable!"

"Thomas!"

"Don't you Thomas me – you wicked bitch!" His voice was like steel. He was so angry with his mother he could have strangled her. Instead, he turned swiftly and left the room, slamming the door behind him. Pulling his jacket round him, he grabbed up his bag, stormed across the large hall and out of the main doors, not seeing his grandparents staring at him from the bottom of the grand staircase.

Thomas ran down the steps and along the side of the house to the garage that housed his car. He took out a bunch of keys – pointed one at the garage door to see it slowly rise, and the car doors unlock. Within seconds Thomas was in his car. He fired the engine with shaking hands. It purred softly. He then switched on his car's computer and tapped in his whereabouts and destination, and a route flashed up onto the screen. He eased his car out of the garage and drove towards the wrought iron gates – a touch of a button in his car opened them – and Thomas roared out.

Emma watched him sadly from the hall window, seeing her dear grandson's sleek red Jaguar flying along the winding, rising lane. With her lips set, she marched into the drawing room to face her daughter. Joanna glared at her mother.

"I know... don't say it...I know."

"You are a fool, Joanna. I warned you this would happen!"

"I know. I know!"

"It was a stupid thing to do – and you should never have had him followed. You cannot keep him tied to your apron strings for ever."

"I know. I know."

"You also know that Thomas is a thoughtful and sensitive person, like Henry and Amy. If he had been different you may have got away with it. All you have done is make him feel guilty, and he will probably spend the rest of his young life trying to make it up to them!"

"What am I going to do?" Joanna's face was full of anguish.

"First of all you will have to apologise!"

"Apologise!"

Yes. Apologise to him – say how sorry you are – and then think of a damn good reason for not telling him about Henry and Penny."

"Very well, Mother."

"And don't ring him now. It might be dangerous ringing whilst he's driving."

"Driving?" Joanna was alarmed.

"He's taken his car."

"He's what!"

"You heard me. He's taken his car."

"How dare he!"

"Now, Joanna, it is his car."

"If you didn't give him such a generous allowance, Mother, he wouldn't have so much freedom."

“He deserves it Joanna – he’s a good boy.”

“You spoil him.”

“Can I suggest,” said Emma firmly,” that you ring Thomas in the morning when you have both cooled down.”

“Very well,” sighed Joanna. Emma turned and left the room gracefully. She was very upset.

Joanna glared at her mother’s retreating back. She was furious with her son and with her mother. She thought of Sally, and blamed her totally for telling Thomas about the Kendals. She thought of the photos that Mr. Abercrombie had sent of Sally and Thomas’s friends. She hated them all!

She did not like being beaten. She paced up and down the room until she stopped at the sight of her late husband’s photo. “What would you do, darling?” she whispered. A smile of devious satisfaction crept into her face as she picked up her mobile phone.

“Mr. Abercrombie? Mrs. Kendal here.”

“Good day, Mrs. Kendal, and what can I do for you?”

“I want you to keep up the surveillance on my son. He now has his car with him. It is a red Jaguar. The number is TK 1.”

“Is that everything?”

“Not quite. That dreadful girl who comes from Cropwell, that my son is friendly with. If she gets too friendly with him, I want you to get rid of her.”

“We don’t deal in murder, Mrs. Kendal.”

“I don’t mean murder,” she trilled. “I just want her frightened off a little.”

“It will cost you, Mrs. Kendal.”

“That’s quite alright. Good day.” Joanna put down the phone and smiled.

When Thomas left Westlake Manor he was shaking with anger. How dare his mother have him followed. What a nerve! He was so upset, he had stormed out of the house on his grandmother’s birthday. He would ring her the next day and apologise.

As he drove along the winding, leafy lanes, a mist began to fall, and Thomas felt he was driving though a cloud. He put on his infa–

red lights and window heaters and slowed down. The weather got steadily worse, the windscreen struggling to keep the wet, cloying mist at bay.

His computer suddenly flashed. There had been an accident ahead, and a new route flashed up onto the screen, which meant he had to detour many miles out of his way. His journey back to Oxford was long and slow, and by the time he reached the Park and Ride car park, it was already getting dark. He locked the car, set the alarm, and made his way to the taxi rank. By the time he got back to his flat it was 6 p.m. He dumped his bag on the kitchen table. He was tired, hungry, and depressed.

Thomas didn't feel like being on his own, so he rang Gus on his mobile.

"Gus. It's Thomas. Where are you?"

"Hi, Tom. We're in The Mitre in High Street. Why what's up?"

"I'm back. Wait for me and I'll join you."

"OK, Tom. See you." Thomas left his flat. He zipped up his jacket, and pulled up his collar. The mist had turned into fine drizzle and he felt damp and cold.

Gus and Kal were talking. They were worried about Thomas.

"But, Gus, why is Thomas back already? He only went to visit his mother this morning, and he was not due back until tomorrow."

"I don't know, Kal. I'm worried about our Tom. It was a terrible shock finding out about those grandparents of his in Cropwell. My guess is that he's had a row with his mother."

"I think you are right. Thomas is very fond of Mr. and Mrs. Kendal and his Aunt Amy. He says they are very nice people, and they have invited us to visit."

"I know, Kal. I think we should go." agreed Gus, looking down at his upper arm to admire his new tattoo of a dinosaur.

"So do I. Here he is!" They looked up as Thomas came into the pub. He looked cold, wet, and miserable.

"Hi, Tom!" shouted Gus, "we're over here!" Thomas threaded his way through the crowded pub, which smelled of food.

"Hi, fellers," greeted Thomas.

"Thomas, my friend, what is wrong?" asked Kal. His brown eyes serious. Thomas joined his two friends at the table.

"I've had a blazing row with my mother."

"What happened, Tom?" asked Gus.

"She's been having me followed."

"Followed?"

"Yes, followed. She knows everywhere I've been, and everything I've done"

"She knows you have been to Cropwell?"

"Yes."

"I'll bet she was fuming."

"She was. She just yelled and screamed at me."

"What did you say?"

"I told her she was a wicked bitch, and stormed out of the house." Gus shook his head.

"Your mother takes some beating – what an old cow!"

"I know. I've never spoken to her like that in my whole life. It was awful!" Thomas's hands were shaking.

"You need a drink, Tom," stated Gus, unfolding his long body from the chair. He got up and went to the bar and brought back three bottles of lager. Thomas put the bottle into his mouth, gratefully, and took a few swigs.

"That's better!" he grinned, and wiped his mouth with the back of his hand. He looked across at his friends. "Well, at least I've got my car!"

"Good for you, Tom!"

The three lads sat drinking and chatting. Thomas was beginning to feel light-headed – he had not eaten since breakfast.

"I'm starving," said Thomas, "let's eat." The lads poured over the menu. "I think I'll have steak, mushrooms and chips," declared Thomas.

"I will have fish and chips – I love the English fish and chips," stated Kal

"I'll have chicken curry and rice," decided Gus, "and a bowl of chips."

They ordered their meals, and carried on drinking whilst they were waiting. Their meals finally arrived, and they tucked in hungrily, then Thomas bought more drinks.

By 11.30 Thomas was falling asleep at the table – he was tired and drunk. Gus and Kal took Thomas back to his flat in a taxi – a two-minute journey. When they got to Thomas's door, Gus held on to Thomas whilst Kal fished round in his pockets for his keys. His two friends got Thomas into his flat, and between them they undressed him and put him to bed.

Thomas slept like a baby.

He slept late the next morning, and woke up with a hangover. He eventually dragged himself out of bed, still wondering how he had got in it in the first place. He showered and dressed, and made his way to the kitchen where he made himself some toast and coffee. He was sitting at the kitchen table going over the events of the day before, when his mobile rang. He fetched it from the bedroom and answered it. It was his mother! He sat down on the bed, his temper rising.

"Thomas, darling, it's me. – I do hope I'm not disturbing you." Her voice was sweet and gentle.

"Hello, Mother. What do you want?"

"Thomas – I'm so sorry about yesterday, darling. I didn't mean to upset you – will you forgive me?"

"Why didn't you tell me about Henry, Penny and Amy?"

"I'm sorry about that, Thomas. It's all my fault, I know. I have been very selfish," she cooed sweetly. "The trouble is, Thomas, that when your father died I was truly heartbroken, and when I realised I was having a baby I was so thrilled, I just didn't want to share you with anyone. I was so afraid that if Henry and Penny knew about you they would demand to see you, and would probably want to take you back to Cropwell for holidays and visits, and I just couldn't let you go. I loved you so much. You do understand, don't you, darling?"

"Yes, Mother, I understand, but you could have told me as I got older."

"I know, darling, it was naughty of me, but the longer I left it the harder it got, and the Kendals did live a long way away, and I wasn't even sure you would want to see them. Anyway, Thomas, you go and see them whenever you wish, and give my apologies to Henry and Penny."

"Very well, Mother."

"We are still friends, aren't we, Thomas?" she asked wistfully.

"Yes, Mother, of course, but I don't want anyone following me about, is that clear?"

"Of course, darling. I'm sorry about that, too. It won't happen again, I promise, "she lied sweetly.

After his mother had rung off Thomas got up from the bed and walked back into the kitchen shaking his head. Could he believe his mother? Whether he did or not he knew he would never forgive her.

The rest of the week flew by, and as it was Henry's birthday on the 1st March, Thomas and Sally went down to Cropwell for the weekend. They had bought him a cherry tree for his back garden, and laid it carefully down on the back seat of Thomas's car.

When Thomas arrived in Cropwell he was greeted warmly, as usual, by Henry and Penny, as they were always thrilled to see him. Henry was pleased with his tree, and Thomas agreed to help him plant it during the weekend.

On the Saturday night, Henry, Penny and Thomas went into Cropwell for a Chinese meal with Amy and Joel. They had a banquet meal and spent the evening nibbling away at all the courses, and enjoying a drink.

Thomas found himself sitting next to Amy at their round table. Thomas liked his aunt very much and was uncertain how to approach her to find out something about his father. He took a chance and spoke to her.

"Aunt Amy, what was my father like?" She looked at him, and once again he saw the fear in her eyes.

"Well, Thomas, he was very kind to me when I was a little girl. He used to play with me and read me stories – but he was quite a few years older than me and once he went to university I didn't see him much, and when he went to live in London, I hardly saw him at all."

Thomas nodded. He felt more puzzled that ever. If Amy hardly ever saw his father as he got older, how could she have found out something terrible about him? Nothing made sense.

Thomas enjoyed the weekend and promised his grandparents he would stay with them during the Easter break.

When Easter arrived, Thomas went down to Cropwell as promised. He was, by now, getting to know his way about, and made friends with the local people. One of the friends Thomas made was Victor Smith, one of the sons of the local farmer. Thomas and Victor would often go riding together on the fields belonging to the farm.

During his visit his grandparents took him to Melton Mowbray to visit Amy and Joel.

"You'll love Amy's home, Thomas, it's so unusual. She and Joel bought a great big old barn and converted it into a house."

The three of them set off one sunny morning. As they approached Melton Mowbray they came to a sharp bend, as they drove round it they saw Amy's unusual house standing between tall, graceful trees, and set behind a neat lawn. The house was called 'Brents Barn'. Arched windows and old oak beams were set in a wall of old, warm red bricks, partly covered in Virginia creeper. A large wooden door with enormous iron hinges was set in the middle. To the right was a smaller building, the bottom half housing three garages, and the top half a flat, housing the married couple who worked for Amy and Joel. The husband was the gardener-cum-handyman, and the wife the cook/housekeeper.

Joel and Amy met them at the door.

"I like your house, Aunt Amy," smiled Thomas.

"Come on, I'll show you round." Whilst Joel took Henry and Penny into the lounge, Amy showed Thomas her home.

Immediately on going through the front door was a long corridor which ran the width of the house, with a winding staircase at each end, leading up to a balcony which ran all round the house. Bedrooms, bathroom, cupboards and Joel's office leading off it. Beside the front door was a telephone with a TV screen at the side. This doubled as a security screen, attached to hidden cameras outside the house, and a screen for showing the person who was telephoning them. The new 'picture–phones' were now becoming popular.

Along the corridor were doors leading to the lounge, dining room, and kitchen. All these rooms faced the back garden through large glass patio doors, leading onto a curved patio, where comfortable garden chairs and tubs of flowers were strewn. The large walled garden was filled with curved lawns, trees in blossom, shrubs, flowers and rockeries. In the centre was a large fish pond, dotted with water lilies in bud. At the bottom of the garden was another patio with a summerhouse on the left, a wrought iron table and chairs in the middle, and a covered barbecue on the right. The whole effect was breathtaking.

All the rooms had smooth wooden ceilings and floors with scatter rugs, and walls of soft pink brick. The furnishings and curtains were of pale green. The lounge was large with an antique desk and bookcase and coffee tables, large plants stood on the floor in big pots, and the room was decorated with beautiful oil paintings, vases of silk flowers and unusual ornaments that Amy and Joel had picked up on their travels abroad. A large, soft leather three piece suite faced a TV in the corner, and a huge open fire place, which led into the dining room. Either side of the fireplace was a wall of Georgian glass, the small wooden squares blending with the floors.

The dining room consisted of a large table surrounded by eight chairs, and a cabinet stretching the width of the room, opposite the fireplace. It was filled with glasses and ornaments and plants. A large bowl of fresh flowers stood in the middle of the table, and a large tree-like plant stood in one corner.

The kitchen was large and fully fitted with wooden units, a table and chairs by the patio doors where Amy and Joel would often sit when they were on their own. The brick walls were decorated with copper pans. Saucepans and kitchenware were all in dark green, and a tall vase of bulrushes stood in a corner. A large window was set between the wall cupboards, overlooking the side of the house. The window had a roller blind covered in rabbits, and expensive pottery rabbits decorated the sill.

Thomas enjoyed his visit to Amy's home, it certainly was different from Westlake Manor!

One day Henry and Penny took Thomas to London for a weekend. Thomas was thrilled as he had always wanted to go, but his mother had refused point blank to visit London. She said it held too many sad memories.

Henry and Penny showed Thomas the house where his parents had lived in Knightsbridge. They also took him to Kendwrick House, where his father was killed, and finally they took him to the churchyard to see his father's grave. They all stood in silence before the large headstone, and Penny laid some flowers on her son's grave. The tears in her eyes made Thomas very conscious of the love that Penny had had for his dead father.

Thomas thought how strange it was that that he felt closer to his father when he was with Henry and Penny, than he had ever felt at home with his mother.

What was the mystery surrounding Thomas Kendal snr.?

CHAPTER EIGHT

MYSTERY - 2012

It was now May, and one lovely sunny weekend Thomas took Gus and Kal down to Cropwell. It was agreed that Gus and Kal would stay the night with Henry and Penny, and Thomas would stay the night at Jade Cottage, with Joel and Amy.

The three lads set off in Thomas's car on the Saturday morning, all looking smart in their clean T–shirts and jeans. Thomas had arranged to call in at Jade Cottage first, to leave his overnight bag. The lads were going in to Cropwell that evening for a pub–crawl, and would be using taxis, Thomas's car being left at his grandparents house.

They arrived in Bishops Fell at 11a.m. The village looked beautiful in the May sunshine. The trees were bursting with foliage, and gardens were full of colour, with pansies and aubretia trailing over stone walls. The church spire gleamed in the sun, and the grey stone cottages looked quaint with their sparkling windows and thatched roofs.

"What a cute little place," grinned Gus.

"It is very beautiful, Thomas, like a place of history," breathed Kal.

They drew up outside Amy's cottage. Thomas was pleased to show his friends his new-found family, and proud that they both admired the lovely village of Bishops Fell. The lads got out of the car, and Thomas picked up his overnight bag. He walked up to the door and rang the bell.

Amy opened the door, looking attractive in navy jeans and a designer T-shirt – her fair hair shining round her pretty face. Amy was growing very fond of Thomas, and greeted him warmly.

"Hello, Thomas, how are you?" Thomas kissed her cheek.

"Hello, Aunt Amy. I would like you to meet my friends – this is Gus, the tall thin one, and this is Kal, the good-looking one!" Amy laughed.

“Hello, Gus, nice to meet you – and you, too, Kal.”

“Amy took them into the cottage and through to the living room, where she introduced them to Joel, who also made them feel welcome. Amy made them all coffee, and they sat chatting in the warmth of the sun as it poured through the windows. Gus and Kal admired the cottage, and Amy told Thomas to show his friends round.

Upstairs were two bedrooms – one facing the road, and one facing the back garden. The bedrooms had low ceilings and heavy, oak beams and were beautifully decorated with matching wallpaper, curtains and bed linen. The front bedroom, Joel and Amy’s, was decorated in peach. The back bedroom had a single bed and was decorated in shades of blue. Next to the back bedroom was a bathroom, which had been added on to the cottage whilst Amy’s grandmother had been living there. On the landing there was a recess with a window, looking out over the carport. In the recess was an ottoman covered in scatter cushions.

There was a winding staircase from the landing leading to a corner of the living room, by the window, and shut off by an old wooden door.

The living room was warm and cosy. It also had a low ceiling and oak beams. The carpet was in green, the two two-seater settees were of peach leather, and the curtains and scatter cushions in a pretty mix of peach, cream and green. The mullioned bay window boasted a window seat, with a vase of expensive silk flowers on the sill. The life-like gas fire was set in a stone fireplace. The TV was in the corner, by the window, and in the other corner was a unit of dark wood, with sparkling glasses, expensive ornaments, and plants. Drinks were kept in the cupboard below. There were oil paintings on the cream walls, and a nest of oak coffee tables stood in the middle of the room, and large plants in pots stood on the floor.

Next to the lounge was a stone passage, with a coat cupboard at one end opposite the door, and a phone on the wall. Off the passage was another bathroom, directly beneath the one upstairs. Next to this was a fitted kitchen in green. The sink under the window which looked out over the back garden. A green table and four chairs stood near the door.

Gus and Kal enjoyed their tour of the cottage, although they had to bend their heads as they went through the doorways. Before they left Amy showed them the garden. The sun was on their faces as they looked round with interest. The back garden had a circular lawn surrounded with flowers. The bottom of the small garden was divided in two. One half was a patio where Amy and Joel had their barbecues, and the other half was taken up by a brick building, which was now the shed, but many years ago had been the outside toilet.

"Outside toilet!" gasped Kal.

"Oh, yes, " laughed Amy. "Many years ago all the houses had outside toilets as there was no plumbing. When my Gran first lived here, she had to go to the village well for water."

"How did people bathe?" asked Kal, amazed.

"They had a tin bath in the kitchen!" replied Amy. Kal shook his head in disbelief. Gus with his knowledge of history, just nodded.

Thomas, Gus and Kal finally said their farewells to Amy and Joel, and made their way to Cropwell. Joel had lent Thomas a spare key, in case he got in late. In ten minutes they had arrived at the Kendal's home in Cropwell.

The house was a large semi-detached in grey stone, with Georgian windows and a large porch. The front garden was like Amy's, with a low stone wall and a neat lawn surrounded by flowers. They all walked up to the front door, which was opened by Thomas's smiling grandparents.

"Hello lads, come on in. Dump your bags anywhere," smiled Henry. They all walked into the hall where they met Penny, who was bubbling with excitement.

"Thomas, it's lovely to see you again, dear." Thomas hugged Penny and kissed her cheek.

"Hello, Grandmother, I'd like you to meet my friends. This is Gus."

Penny shook hands with Gus. She looked up at him. "My goodness, you're so tall!" Gus grinned.

"It has its disadvantages, Mrs. Kendal, I keep banging my head." Penny chuckled happily.

"And this is Kal," said Thomas.

Penny looked at Kal, noticing his black wavy hair, his coffee coloured skin, warm brown eyes and even white teeth.

"Hello, Kal, you look just like Omar Shariff without a moustache!"

"Thank you, Mrs. Kendal," smiled Kal, taking her hand and kissing her fingers. Penny blushed, and everyone laughed.

"I guess you must all be hungry," rejoined Henry. "As the weather is so warm today we are having a barbecue for lunch." Henry led everyone outside to the long back garden, which was lawned and surrounded by flowers and trees. There were lilac trees in full bloom and peonies full of deep pink flowers, nodding in the sun.

Henry had laid out comfortable garden chairs for them all. As they sat down Henry put some steaks on to the prepared grill, along with chicken legs and kebabs on sticks. Penny brought out some cans of cold lager for them to drink whilst they were waiting. When the meat was ready Penny brought out a dish of small new potatoes with butter melting on the top, and a large dish of salad.

They all spent a pleasant afternoon in the garden, replete after their delicious meal. They were all happy and relaxed, and Thomas felt the usual warm contentment he always had when he was with Henry and Penny.

At 7.30 that evening Henry gave the three lads a lift into the town centre. Cropwell, like Oxford, had a mixture of old and new pubs and bars. The lads moved from one to another. The pubs and bars were full of young people like themselves, and they had a good time chatting, joking and laughing.

At 11.30, all a bit merry, they made their way to an Indian restaurant, where they all tucked into hot, spicy food, and had more to drink.

When they were ready to go, one of the waiters rang for a taxi, and they all bundled in. Thomas was giggling, and Gus and Kal were doing their best to shut him up. When they got to Henry's, Gus and Kal got out and paid the fare to the driver, who then took Thomas to Bishops Fell.

When Thomas got out of the taxi he staggered happily up to the front door, and groped for the key that Joel had given him. Although the cottage appeared to be in darkness, Joel had left a light on in the passage. Thomas bolted the door, and with fumbling fingers turned off the light and tottered through the living room towards the door at the bottom of the stairs.

As he approached the door he fell over and landed on his hands and knees, he then swore as he banged his head against the wall. As he was struggling to get up, Thomas felt a hard lump on the carpet, under his hand. He frowned. "Wassat?" he mumbled to himself. He eventually got to his feet and walked uncertainly to put on the light. He went back to the corner of the room, but could see nothing. He bent down and lifted up the corner of the carpet, and stared in surprise. Sunk into the floor, in the corner of the room, was a safe. Thomas stared at it and frowned. It was a small safe of grey steel. There was no fancy dial on it – just a keyhole and a small handle for lifting up the door.

What on earth was it doing here? Surely if Joel and Amy had any valuables or money, they would have been kept in the safe at 'Brents Barn'. They were only at the cottage at weekends. Thomas's heart missed a beat. Could the secret of his father's past be hidden in that safe? He was certain that Amy knew.

His face suddenly serious, he laid the carpet back in place, switched off the light, and opened the stairs door, trying not to rattle the old–fashioned metal catch. He crept slowly up the winding stairs, cursing as each one creaked under his feet. He made his way to the back bedroom, kicked off his shoes, dropped his clothes on the floor, and wearing only his underpants, climbed into bed. The moment his head touched the pillow, he was asleep.

Thomas woke the next morning to find his room filled with a dusky light. The curtains were open, as he had forgotten to draw them the night before. The sunshine from the day before had gone, and he lay there watching the raindrops tapping against the window. He lay in bed feeling warm and comfortable until nature called. He crawled out of bed and went to the bathroom to relieve himself. He heard movements downstairs, and realised that Joel and Amy were up, so he showered and dressed and made his way downstairs.

"Good morning, Thomas," smiled Amy. "Have a good evening?"

"Yes, thanks," he grinned sheepishly. "Too much drink, and sorry about the garlic!"

"I wondered where the funny smell was coming from," laughed Joel.

"You OK with bacon sandwiches, Thomas? We don't keep a lot of food here being away all week."

"That will be great, thanks."

Amy set about getting breakfast and making coffee, and Joel and Thomas sat chatting at the kitchen table.

"I do like your cottage, Aunt Amy. Promise me if you ever sell it, I can have first offer!"

"If you are very good," teased Amy, "I will leave it to you in my will. I would like it kept in the family."

"So would I," he replied, "and I can leave it to my children, if I have any."

Thomas did not miss the look of alarm that passed between his aunt and her husband.

After breakfast Thomas collected his bag, and Joel gave him a lift to Henry's and Penny's. When Joel got back he found Amy in he kitchen taking a couple of painkillers.

"Amy, what's wrong?"

"I'm getting those pains in my stomach again."

"Amy you must see a doctor."

"I know. But they do go away, and then I feel alright." Joel walked up to her and put his hands on her slender shoulders.

"Amy. I couldn't bear it if anything happened to you, you know that."

"I promise I'll see a doctor."

"Good girl." He put his arms round her and hugged her tightly.

When Thomas got to his grandparent's house, they were all in the kitchen. Henry, Gus and Kal were all chatting animatedly round the kitchen table. Penny was pottering round the kitchen, happy to be surrounded by a group of handsome men!

During the morning, as the rain had ceased, Henry took the lads for the usual walk through the woods, ending up at the Fox and Hounds for a drink.

When they got back they tucked into one of Penny's mouth-watering Sunday dinners, and spent the afternoon lazing about, chatting until it was time for Thomas and his friends to go back to Oxford. Thomas was anxious to get back and tell Sally about the hidden safe. She had stayed at Oxford that weekend to visit a concert with some friends.

The three lads climbed into Thomas's car, and Henry and Penny waved to them from the doorway. Gus sat in the front, as there was more room for his long legs, and Kal sat sedately in the back. Gus wriggled in his seat to get comfortable, and pushing his glasses along his nose he spoke to Thomas.

"Your grandparents are great, Tom, it's no wonder you like to come and see them so often."

"They are indeed," piped up Kal from the back seat.

"Henry is so good to talk to, and so knowledgeable. I wish my old man would find time to talk to me like he does."

"He must have been a very good teacher, Thomas."

"I believe he was, Kal. I often wish he was my father," replied Thomas, wistfully.

Whilst the lads were making their way back to Oxford, Joel and Amy remembered that they had promised to ring Andrew Shaw again and tell him about Thomas. Joel rang the number and heard it ring for some time before it was answered.

"Could I speak to Andrew Shaw, please?"

"I am Mrs. Shaw. I'm afraid my husband is not well at the moment, he is in hospital. Can I take a message to him?"

"Could you just tell him that Joel Brent rang, and that everything seems fine. He will know what I mean."

"Yes, of course."

"Thank you. If he needs to ring me, he knows the number, and I can transfer messages from it."

"Very well, Mr. Brent, Goodbye."

"Goodbye, Mrs. Shaw."

Amy had been listening. "Well, we have rung. If he wants to speak to us he can ring."

Andrew Shaw never did.

When the lads arrived in Oxford it had started raining again. As they parked the car Thomas decided to ring Sally, using the mobile in his car he rang her.

"Sally, it's Thomas. We've just got back. Can I see you?"

"Of course, I'm in the Wig and Pen. We've just been to the Apollo to see another concert."

"I'll see you shortly."

"OK, Thomas. Bye."

After locking and securing the car they caught a taxi into Oxford. Gus and Kal were dropped off at their flat, and the driver took Thomas to his. Thomas asked the driver to wait whilst he took his overnight bag up to his flat. The taxi then took him to the Wig and Pen. Thomas paid the driver and ran through the rain into the pub. He soon found her sitting with some friends.

"Hi, Sally."

"Hi, Thomas. Have a good weekend?"

"Great thanks. Can we talk?" Sally noticed the urgency in his voice, and got up. They walked out of the pub, and Sally put up her large umbrella. Thomas put his arm round her shoulders as they walked slowly along together, under the steady patter of rain above their heads. Thomas told Sally about the hidden safe at Amy's.

"What do you think, Sally?"

"You could be right, Thomas. They would certainly be more likely to have a safe in their house at Melton Mowbray. Perhaps Amy's Gran put in the safe."

"Of course, I never thought of that!"

The two of them walked on, still discussing the mystery of Amy's safe.

CHAPTER NINE

ATTEMPTED MURDER? – 2012

The weeks flew by and the summer break had arrived. Sally had now finished her first year at Oxford and Thomas his second.

Sally and her friend were going touring in Europe. They wanted to practise their languages and work as waitresses to earn some pocket money as they went along. Sally agreed to meet Thomas in Cropwell at the end of August.

For the first week of the holiday Thomas went home to Westlake Manor. He did not want to see his mother particularly, but felt guilty about not seeing his grandparents. He had only been home a couple of days when Joanna flew off to their villa at La Manga Club in Spain. She was angry with Thomas when he refused to go with her, but had managed to control her temper, not wanting another row with her son.

Thomas did not have many friends at home, his mother had seen to that over the years. He spent some time with Marcus and Emma before going to Portugal to see Kal, and then going to Cropwell to stay with Henry and Penny and meet up with Sally.

During his week at home Thomas spent some time with Tim. Tim had been thrilled to see Thomas, his vacant-looking eyes lighting up at the sight of his friend. The two lads went fishing together and played football in the yard of Ben's cottage like a couple of schoolboys, and also went riding together.

A couple of days before he was due to go to Portugal, Thomas had been out riding with Tim, as he strolled back to Westlake Manor he was met by Emma.

"Oh, Thomas, there you are. We have some visitors, do come and say hello." Thomas smiled and followed his grandmother into the house. When Thomas walked into the drawing room he gasped in surprise, for there were Henry and Penny sitting smugly on the sofa, grinning.

"What on earth are you doing here?" he exclaimed. Henry and Penny laughed.

"Emma and Marcus invited us for a few days," smiled Penny.

"Well, Thomas, whilst the cat's away..." laughed Emma.

"Grandmother, you are incorrigible!" He went over to Penny and kissed her cheek, and shook Henry's hand. "It's lovely to see you both, I can't believe you are here."

"We thought it would be nice for us to have a get-together," added Marcus.

"I think it's a wonderful idea," laughed Thomas, "but I am going to Portugal in a couple of days..."

"That's alright, Thomas," said Henry, cheerfully, "You go and enjoy yourself, you don't want to be stuck here with us old fogies!"

Thomas spent the weekend with his two sets of grandparents. It seemed strange to see them all together, but a relief to see that they were all on good terms, after Joanna's attempt to keep them apart.

Thomas spent the next two weeks in Portugal with Kal and his family, and once again had a wonderful holiday with this charming family. By the end of the fortnight Thomas was relaxed and sun-tanned. He flew to Birmingham and picked up his car, and drove down to Cropwell for the rest of the summer. Thomas had many friends there now, and would go riding and fishing and sometimes play tennis. He often helped Henry in the garden and would take Penny shopping. He was looking forward to seeing Sally. They had become good friends, and he was growing to like her very much.

By the end of August Sally was home, looking sun-tanned and happy. Her soft, curly hair had grown quite long and was now tied up on top of her head, with soft tendrils falling round her ears. The hairstyle showed up her heart–shaped face.

Thomas hugged Sally when they met.

"You look terrific, Sally, I've missed you."

"I've missed you, too, Thomas," she smiled.

The two of them had the whole of September to spend together, although Sally had got herself a part-time job as a waitress at Gino's, an Italian restaurant in Cropwell town centre. She wanted to practise her Italian and earn some pocket money. She always refused to accept money from Thomas.

One Friday, early in the evening, Sally had gone to work, dressed smartly in her white blouse and black skirt and sensible shoes. She parked her mother's car and walked along the street to the restaurant. She stood at the kerb, and making sure the road was clear, she started to cross to the other side. Suddenly, there was a screech of tyres, and to her horror, Sally saw a large black car racing towards her. It hit her, throwing her against a delivery van which was parked on the double yellow lines. The black car sped off leaving Sally lying in the road, a pool of blood slowly forming under her head.

Some shocked passers by rushed to her aid, one of them using a mobile phone to call an ambulance and the police.

The crowd around her was talking.

"That was deliberate – he tried to kill her!"

"We musn't move her – she's banged her head."

"Is she still alive?"

The crowd round Sally grew – some of them holding back the traffic, as Sally was lying in the middle of the road.

Sirens were screaming as an ambulance arrived, followed by a police car. Two paramedics leapt out of the ambulance and ran to her, and began to examine her gently.

"She's still alive."

"She's broken her left arm."

Sally was laid carefully on to a stretcher, strapped down and put into the ambulance, which drove slowly away. They took her to the new accident department of Cropwell General Hospital.

The police cordoned off the road and took photographs, and questioned people in the crowd, and took statements from witnesses.

Gino was shocked when he realised that it was Sally who had been run over, and rang Molly and Richard. They went round to tell Thomas, but he was out. Henry and Penny were horrified when they heard what had happened to Sally. Thomas had gone horse riding with Victor Smith at Cropwell Farm.

"Shall we ring him, Henry?" asked Penny, her hazel eyes anxious.

"We'll wait 'til he gets home, Pen. There's nothing he can do at the moment, and they won't let him see her yet. He'll be home in a couple of hours. We'll ring the hospital then and find out the situation."

"Oh, dear," whispered Penny tearfully, "I do hope she'll be alright."

"Don't worry, Pen," soothed Henry, patting her hand. "I'm sure she'll be fine."

A short while later Richard rang to say that Sally would be alright. She had cuts and bruises and a broken arm. She'd had a scan, and there were no internal injuries or brain damage.

"Thank God!" cried Penny.

"Richard said Sally is in the theatre having her arm set."

"Shall we ring Thomas now?"

"Yes, we will."

Thomas was on his way home when Henry rang. He came rushing into the house, full of questions. Henry and Penny told him all they knew.

"A hit and run!" he exclaimed. "She could have been killed!"

"She's been very lucky," replied Henry.

"I'll go and see her now." Thomas rushed out, climbed into his car, and tore off to the hospital.

Thomas soon arrived at Cropwell General. He cursed under his breath as he had difficulty in finding a space in the car park. He eventually found a space as another car departed. He parked and locked his Jag and marched purposefully through the rows of cars to the building.

He was so worried about Sally, he did not notice the glorious sun setting behind the trees, turning the leaves to gold, or the myriads of light sparkling on the hospital windows.

Thomas strode through the main doors and up to the reception desk. His fair hair was tousled and he was still wearing his sweater, jeans and old riding boots that he had borrowed from Victor Smith. Thomas stood restlessly in the queue until it was his turn. He spoke to the receptionist, his face lined with worry.

"I've come to see Sally Bennett. She was in a road accident earlier this evening, in Cropwell."

"I'll just check for you," she replied, kindly, picking up the phone.

"She's just come out of theatre, and has been taken to ward D2." She told Thomas how to get there.

"Thank you." Thomas marched over to the lifts. He waited restlessly until it arrived. He got in and pressed the button for the second floor, and soon found himself in a large corridor. Molly and Richard were sitting on chairs looking lost and unhappy. They looked up.

"Thomas, it's so good of you to come."

"How is she?"

"She's going to be alright. She has broken her arm, and has cuts and bruises on her face and legs. She's just been taken to the ward, and we should be able to see her soon," said Richard.

"A policewoman has been up, but as she couldn't see Sally yet, she's coming back tomorrow," added Molly.

"What happened," asked Thomas. Richard frowned.

"She was crossing the road to Gino's when a large black car hit her and drove off. The policewoman told us that the witnesses thought it was deliberate. But who would want to hurt Sally?"

"I've no idea," frowned Thomas, shaking his head in bewilderment.

A nurse came out of Sally's ward, which contained four beds.

"You can see you daughter now. She is still rather sleepy," she said to the Bennetts.

"Thank you, nurse," they replied.

Thomas, Molly and Richard filed into the ward. Sally was lying in a bed by the window. Her face was white. A huge black bruise covered her left temple and her eye was swollen. She had small cuts over her face, from the gravel on the road, the blood turning brown. Her soft brown curls lay limp on the pillow.

Her left arm was in a sling, weighed down by the heavy plaster. Her body was covered in a white hospital gown.

The three of them approached the bed, ignoring the patients in two of the other beds. Thomas sat down beside the bed and took Sally's hand, his inside churning. Molly and Richard sat on the other side and gazed at their only daughter, lying pale and still. Thomas' face was lined with worry as he gently stroked her hand. They sat in silence praying for her to wake up.

After what seemed an eternity Sally finally opened her eyes. Her left eye was bloodshot, and she blinked.

"Hello, Sally, how are you feeling?"

"Hello, Mum, a bit woosy." She saw Thomas and smiled weakly. "Hello, Thomas."

"Hi, Sally, what have you been up to?" he smiled.

"Can't remember..." she drifted back to sleep."

Thomas continued to sit with Sally. He agreed to stay whilst Richard and Molly went to collect Molly's car from the car park near Gino's, and get Sally a nightdress and some toiletries from home, and bring them to the hospital.

After their return to the hospital, Sally woke up again, and they were able to talk to her, but a nurse soon arrived and asked them to leave, as it was well past visiting time. Thomas kissed Sally on the cheek before leaving. He would never forget the sight of her injured body.

The following day Sally was inundated with visitors, flowers and get well cards. Thomas stayed with her all day, and Sally's parents and Henry and Penny made long visits. The policewoman returned and took a statement from Sally, whose last memory was of the black car racing towards her. She didn't see the driver. The policewoman told her that the car had been stolen, and found abandoned a few miles away.

When she had gone Sally turned to Thomas. "I thought the driver was trying to kill me. He came straight at me."

"He stole the car, Sally, perhaps he didn't see you until the last minute."

"Yes, that's true."

"How are you feeling now?"

"I hurt all over. How do I look?"

"Like you've just gone ten rounds with Muhammad Ali."

"The boxer?"

"Yes."

"I must look a mess," she grinned.

"Well, not quite as pretty as you looked the other day," he teased, squeezing her hand.

Sally stayed in hospital for two more days, as she had had a head injury. Thomas collected her and drove her carefully home. Molly and Richard fussed over her, and whilst they were both at work Sally stayed at the Kendals, where she was well cared for. Penny was marvellous to her, cutting up her food, bathing her wounds and helping her to the bathroom. When Sally first looked in the mirror she had been horrified at the state of her face. Her bruises were turning into shades of yellow and green and purple, and the swellings had distorted her features.

Thomas fussed over Sally, thankful that she had not been killed, or more seriously hurt.

By the end of September Thomas and Sally were due back at Oxford. Sally's face was almost healed, and although her arm was still in plaster she could still use her right hand, and would be able to study.

"But, Sally," demanded her mother, "how will you get dressed and get meals?"

"It's OK, Mum, my two flat mates will help, I've already phoned them, so don't worry."

Thomas took Sally back to Oxford. They were both glad to be back and meet up with their friends. Sally's flat mates were full of concern over her accident, and helped her all they could.

Thomas and Kal had phoned each other before their return, but Gus, whose uncle was an archaeologist, had been on a 'dig' as usual, during the summer break.

Life at Keble soon got back to normal, and Thomas was approaching his 21st birthday. By 1st November Sally was much better. Her face was now back to it's normal, pretty self, and her arm was healed.

On 1st November Gus and Kal had arranged a surprise party for Thomas at Keble. There was a room laid with a superb buffet, plenty of drink and a 'disco'. Sally looked very glamorous in a long blue dress, her face made up, covering the small scars on her skin, and her hair was a cloud of shining curls.

Thomas had a wonderful evening. He felt happy and carefree. His heart was glowing at the sight of Sally – who was now becoming very special to him.

He had no idea of the horrors that were creeping up behind him.

CHAPTER TEN

A SHOCKING DISCOVERY - NOVEMBER 2012

The weekend following Thomas's 21st birthday he and Sally went down to Cropwell, as Henry and Penny also wanted to celebrate. They arrived on the Saturday morning, and Thomas was greeted by an excited Penny and a cheerful Henry. She gave Thomas a big hug.

"Happy birthday, Thomas!"

"Thank you Grandmother." Penny and Henry had two gifts for Thomas. Penny handed him the first one.

"We do hope you will like it, we had it done specially," she beamed. Thomas opened the flat parcel, and took out a large photograph in a wooden, oval frame. There were four people in the picture. At the back was a picture of a beautiful woman of about 35 years of age with her golden hair piled on top of her head. Next was a young man with fair hair and glasses. Slightly in front was Thomas's father and in front was Thomas himself. Thomas gazed at it in astonishment and looked across at Henry.

"How..?" Henry smiled.

"The picture is your Kendal line. The blonde woman at the back is my mother, Caroline. I don't have a photo of my father, so you've got my mother instead. The man with the glasses is me when I was young.

"It's amazing," gasped Thomas. "It looks as we have all been photographed together – how did you do it?"

"It's a kind of collage, Thomas. I gave all the photos to a photographer and he put them together."

"It's marvellous, thank you, both, very much."

"We've got you this as well, in case you didn't like it," smiled Penny giving him his second gift.

Thomas opened the large box to find a brand new pair of black riding boots, the smell of the rich leather rose to meet him.

"We can't have you going round in those scruffy, old boots of Victor's," stated Penny.

"Thank you very much, they are the perfect gift, both of them are." He bent to kiss Penny's cheek and she blushed happily.

"You've both been very kind to me, and I do appreciate it." Henry patted him on the shoulder.

"You've been good to us, too, Thomas. You've made us both very happy in our old age."

Penny trotted off to the kitchen to make them all coffee. Thomas made her so happy, she always wanted to cry. By the time she returned to the living room with the coffee, she had pulled herself together.

"Thomas," said Henry, "tonight we're going to take you to your favourite Chinese restaurant. Sally and her parents and Joel and Amy will be coming too. I hope that will be alright with you."

"Of course," replied Thomas. "Sounds perfect."

"Thomas," said Penny, "I thought you should know that Amy is going into hospital for an operation."

"What's wrong?" frowned Thomas.

"It's nothing serious, dear. Just a woman's little problem."

"When does she go in?"

"Well, Joel is taking her in tomorrow evening, to a private hospital in Melton, to get her settled in and do her "pre-med" things, then on Monday morning they will take her down to the theatre and put a tiny camera into her to find out exactly what is wrong, and then operate straight away."

"I see," replied Thomas slowly. "I do hope she will be alright."

"Of course she will, dear, now don't you worry."

Thomas was concerned about Amy, but when he saw her that evening he had to admit that she did not look ill, and it did not spoil their enjoyable evening.

After opening gifts from Amy and the Bennetts, they all enjoyed their meal, and afterwards they all went back to Henry's and Penny's for more drinks and chatter. When Joel and Amy left Thomas kissed his aunt and wished her well. He was very fond of Amy and anxious about her going into hospital. The Kendals and the Bennetts had a late night.

Late on the Sunday afternoon Thomas was relaxing with a cup of tea before his journey back to Oxford, when the phone rang.

"Thomas, it's for you," said Henry.

Thomas went into the hall and picked up the receiver.

"Thomas?"

"Yes, Joel, what's up?"

"Thomas, would you mind doing something for me?"

"What is it?"

"We're at home in Melton, and I'm just about to take Amy to the hospital, and she can't find her bunch of keys. She thinks she must have left them at the cottage. Would you mind calling in on your way home and having a look for me?"

"That's no problem."

"Can you call me on my mobile and let me know?"

"Of course. How do I get in?"

"You can borrow Henry's key and leave it in the cottage. I can use my key to get in, and I'll give Henry his back when I see him. Oh, and Amy's keys have a gold A on a chain on the ring."

"OK, Joel. I'll be leaving shortly. I'll ring you soon."

"Thanks, Thomas, goodbye."

"Bye, Joel."

A short time later Thomas and Sally left the Kendal's home and armed with Henry's key set off for Bishop's Fell. Within ten minutes they were inside the cottage where Thomas soon found Amy's keys. They had slipped down the side of the settee. Using his mobile he rang Joel, who answered after many rings.

"Thomas, sorry you had to wait – I've had to come outside the hospital to use my phone. Did you find them?"

"Yes, where shall I put them?"

"There's a drawer in the kitchen with tea-towels in, just put them in there."

"OK, I'll put Henry's key in there, too."

"Thanks, Thomas."

"OK, bye." Thomas rang off. He stood looking down at the bunch of keys lying in his hand.

"Thomas," queried Sally, "what's up?"

"I wonder if the key to that safe is here?"

"Thomas, you mustn't. It would be wrong!"

"I know, but this may be my only chance and, Sally – I've got to know. I won't rest until I know the truth about my father."

"There might be no secrets in there."

"But there could be!" Before his courage could fail him, Thomas knelt down and pulled up the carpet from the corner of the room to reveal the safe. Sally went across and looked over his shoulder. Thomas's heart was hammering as he selected a suitable key – he put it into the lock and turned the key – he heard a 'click' and lifted the door. Inside was a black metal box with a handle on the top.

"Sally, draw the curtains, quick!" He lifted out the box and took it over to the coffee table. Thomas and Sally sat side by side on the settee, and with trembling fingers he began searching for the key. At the second attempt, the box was unlocked. Thomas slowly lifted the lid, and they both peered inside.

"Papers," he whispered.

"We must keep them in order, Thomas."

Thomas slowly lifted out a sheet of folded paper and opened it out.

"It's a family tree!" gasped Sally.

They both stared at it in amazement.

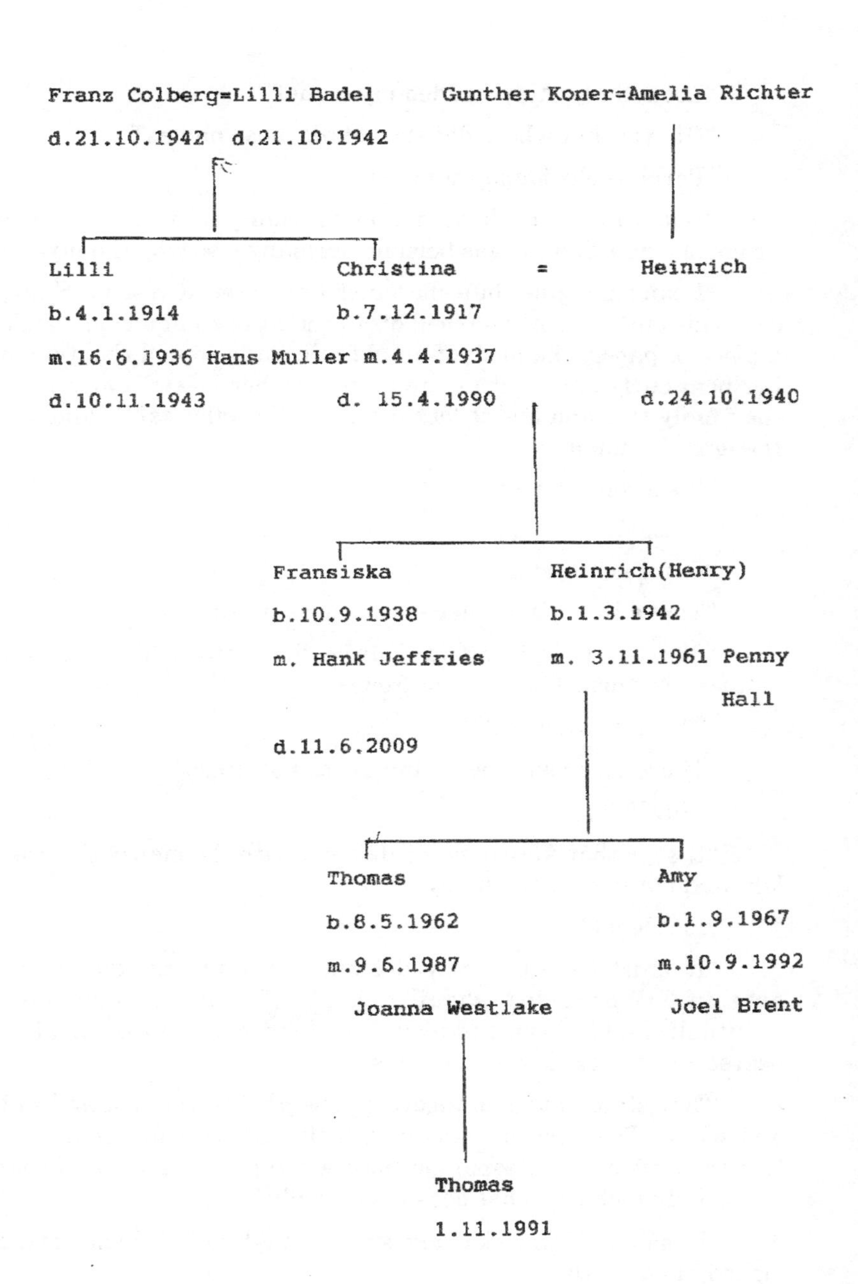
Franz Colberg=Lilli Badel
d.21.10.1942 d.21.10.1942
Gunther Koner=Amelia Richter
Lilli
b.4.1.1914
m.16.6.1936 Hans Muller
d.10.11.1943
Christina
b.7.12.1917
m.4.4.1937
d. 15.4.1990
=
Heinrich
d.24.10.1940
Fransiska
b.10.9.1938
m. Hank Jeffries
d.11.6.2009
Heinrich(Henry)
b.1.3.1942
m. 3.11.1961 Penny Hall
Thomas
b.8.5.1962
m.9.6.1987
Joanna Westlake
Amy
b.1.9.1967
m.10.9.1992
Joel Brent
Thomas
1.11.1991

"Look, Sally, Amy's added my name!"

"Oh, yes, but where did she get all these names?"

"Perhaps she found them here."

"But why keep them a secret? Henry already knows about Fransiska and that he was born in Germany – so why the mystery?"

"I can't imagine, but she must have a good reason. Sally, let's copy this out!" Thomas dashed off to the kitchen and came back with a piece of paper, the back of an old bill. Sally copied the 'tree' out in her neat curly handwriting, and put it in her bag. Thomas folded up the family tree and laid it face down on the coffee table, and took out the next document.

"It's a copy of a will."

"Whose?"

"Caroline Kendal."

"That's Henry's mother – what does it say?"

"She left everything to Amy – the cottage, contents and all monies," he turned it over and frowned.

"Thomas, what is it?"

"There's a proviso here...but...that's strange."

"Why?"

"It says that Amy must be discreet with the money she has been left, and not to give any to my father."

"Is it legal?"

"It must be – but why did she not want my father to have anything? Why didn't she like him?" Thomas was puzzled. He eventually laid it down and picked up a faded old brown envelope. He peered inside. "Look, Sally, photos!"

They stared at them together. The photos were old and in black and white. The first one was of a little girl with fair hair. Thomas turned it over to see some German writing on the back. *'Fransiska meine liebe tochter.'* What does it say, Sally?"

"It means Fransiska, my lovely daughter." Thomas and Sally looked at each other.

"Fransiska? – But surely she was my grandfather's sister. Amy must have known about her all the time – why on earth has she kept it hidden away?"

"I'll bet that's why she fainted when she got back from her honeymoon and Henry told her about his sister turning up. She must have fainted with shock!"

"But why?"

"Let's carry on and find out." They looked at the next photo that was of a little boy with blond curls – on the back was written 'Heinrich'.

"That's the German for Henry, Thomas – this must be your grandfather." Thomas shook his head.

"I can't believe this – Grandfather's photo also hidden away – it doesn't make sense." He laid down the photo of Henry and picked up the next one. It was a fair–haired young woman wearing a silky suit and a big hat, standing beside a man in uniform. It looked like a wedding photo. They turned it over, and on the back was written *'unsere hochzeit tag."*

"This says 'our wedding day' " said Sally. Thomas looked more closely at the photo and frowned.

"I think this woman is Caroline," said Thomas slowly. He told Sally about the photograph that his grandparents had given him for his birthday. "She looks just like Caroline in that photograph."

"In that case, this is a photo of Caroline with her husband, Heinrich."

"So that means that Aunt Amy has had a photo of Grandfather's father all this time. Why has she never shown him?" Thomas was baffled. He picked up the next photo, which was of another young woman laughing. On the back was written *'Lilli meine fraundliche schelster.'*

"This means 'Lilli my dear sister'," said Sally. This lovely young girl was in the next photo. She was wearing a silky dress and coat and a wide-brimmed hat. She was standing with a man in uniform, too. Sally turned it over. On the back was *'Lilli und Hans'*.

"So this is Caroline's sister with her husband," murmured Sally. She picked up the last photo, which was of an elderly couple standing in front of a lovely house. On the back was written *'meine eltern'*.

"This couple are Caroline's parents." Thomas ran a hand through his blond hair.

"These people are all my ancestors, it's incredible." Sally laid the photographs down on top of the pile, whilst Thomas took out the next envelope. Inside was some letters and a list of names all written in German. Thomas handed the list to Sally.

"What does it say?" he asked her urgently. Sally stared at it for a few seconds, then started to translate.

"The word at the top *'eintelen'* means 'contacts'. The first one reads – *Der Artz* – Doctor – Petr Michaels – Harley Street, London. The next one is *'gasthaus besitzer'* – that means 'landlord' – Theodor Schen – Golden Lion – Lime Street, Whitechapel, London. The next is *'Der Kempelbehindler'* – that's an antique dealer – Harold Steel – High Street, Cropwell." Sally frowned.

"What's the matter?" asked Thomas.

"This Harold Steel, the antique dealer – I remember my dad telling me something about the Steel family."

"What was it?"

"Well, the Steel family owned Cropwell Manor for generations. Many years ago Harold Steel died, and the estate was passed on to his son. Years later, for some strange reason, the son sold Cropwell Manor and went to live abroad with his family. Dad said everyone was shocked. Anyway when the estate was finally sold, Cropwell Manor was turned into a private school. It's still very popular today."

"And no-one knows why he left the country?"

"No, it's still a bit of a mystery. Anyway, the next person on this list is *'Der arnwaht'* – solicitor – 24 High Street, Cropwell, and the last one is *'Der lehrer'* – school teacher – Gerald Smith – Bishops Fell. What do you think of that lot, Thomas?" Thomas frowned and rubbed his hands nervously along his thighs.

"I think Caroline Kendal was a German spy."

"A German spy!" gasped Sally, "but why?"

"For one thing – she came over here during the war with Grandfather as a baby and left Fransiska behind. I believe she brought Grandfather with her for 'cover' and left his sister behind, probably because she didn't speak English."

"But why did she stay here?"

"If you look at that family tree chart you will see that Lilli and Hans were killed in 1943, and according to Fransiska, when she was found alone she was taken to America. Caroline must have thought she had been killed, so she decided to stay here."

"It certainly all fits, and Henry would have been growing up here and would only be speaking English. I'll bet all the people on that list were either German spies, too, or English traitors." Sally suddenly gasped. "Of course, that would explain why the Steels left the country – perhaps the son found out about his late father's activities, and was so ashamed he wanted to get away."

"Unless the Special Branch were on to him."

"Special Branch?"

"Yes, maybe Amy sent Andrew Shaw a copy of that list – he's got to fit in somewhere."

"True," replied Sally, "but this list has no connection with your father."

"No," replied Thomas," but I feel as if pieces of a jig–saw are beginning to fall into place."

Sally laid down the list on top of the photos, whilst Thomas picked up 3 fading envelopes all addressed to Mrs. C. Kendal, Jade Cottage, Bishops Fell.

"There are no stamps on these letters, Thomas, they must have been delivered by hand."

"Probably brought over here by another German spy," suggested Thomas. "What do they say, Sally?"

Sally opened out the letters, which were all quite short. "Someone has translated these, " exclaimed Sally.

"That's Joel's writing, I'm sure," murmured Thomas. Heads together they stared at the translations. The letters were all written to Christina (alias Caroline) from her sister Lilli. They were all dated in 1943 and the address was *Perleberstrasse 40*, Berlin. The letters consisted of family chat such as "we hope Heinrich is well" – "Fransiska sends her love" – "Anna has had a baby boy, they are both fine" – "Amelia has a new boyfriend, she is being very naughty and has not been home. She does not know you are in England." In the last letter dated September, 1943, Lilli says that they fear that

Germany is going to lose the war, and they are going to America with friends. Lilli promises that when they arrive they will send Christina the address so that she and Heinrich can go and join them."

"This fits in with Fransiska's story," declared Thomas.

"So Caroline was left here with your grandfather. Just imagine, Thomas, Caroline must have thought her daughter had been killed – she never knew that a couple of years after her own death, her daughter would turn up on Henry's doorstep. How sad!"

Sally put the letters and translations back into their envelopes and added them to the pile.

Thomas picked up the next letters. One was a computer copy dated August, 1990. It had been sent to a German researcher, a Mr. Meyer, asking him to start tracing Caroline's ancestors, and to find the war records of Heinrich Koner (Carolines's husband) and Hans Muller (Lilli's husband). The letter was written by Joel, giving a P.O. Box number for a reply.

The next letter was a reply from Mr. Meyer. He had found the birth of Lilli – her marriage to Hans Muller and their deaths in 1943. He had also found the death of Christina's and Lilli's parents. He had been unable to find the death of Fransiska, and had passed on the research for the army records to another man who had access to the Berlin archives, and was an expert in war history. The next letter was another from Mr. Meyer. It was short and brief – telling Joel that the researcher who had been tracking down the war records of Heinrich and Hans, had been killed in a 'hit and run'. The last letter was a copy from Joel, asking the researcher to stop.

"How awful!" cried Sally. "Amy and Joel must have felt terrible." Thomas nodded in agreement – he was beginning to feel scared and uncomfortable. Sally began to put the letters back into the envelope.

"There's something else in here," and pulled out, gently, two old newspaper cuttings. "Look at these, Thomas!" He stared at them, puzzled.

"What do they say?"

"Oh, no!" she gasped.

"What is it, Sally?"

"This picture is of Henry's father with Adolf Hitler! The picture was taken at a function in Berlin. It says that Heinrich was a close friend of Hitler, and that Heinrich has been killed."

"My God!" gasped Thomas, "my Grandfather's parents were friends of Hitler – it's unbelievable!"

"No wonder Amy's kept quiet about all this – Henry would be horrified if he knew!"

"What does the other one say?" Sally skimmed over the article – her eyes opened wide.

"Sally?"

"This is a picture of Henry's mother, now a widow. She's at a function with Adolf Hitler." Thomas was appalled. He stared at Sally.

"I can't believe all this – where did Amy get it all?"

"She must have found all this when she moved in here."

"What a terrible shock for her." They sat and stared at the newspaper cuttings – neither of them knowing what else to say.

"The phone in the passage suddenly rang. Thomas and Sally froze.

"Don't answer it!" hissed Thomas. They sat like two statues, their hearts pounding, until the phone stopped ringing, Sally picked up the cuttings from where they had fallen on the floor.

"Let's hurry up, Thomas, I'm scared."

"So am I," he replied quietly.

"How many envelopes are left?"

"Just two." Sally put the cuttings back into the envelope with the letters, and added it to the growing pile. Thomas lifted out the next envelope – it was quite heavy. They looked inside and saw a pile of fabric envelopes. Thomas carefully moved the box away and tipped out the fabric envelopes onto the coffee table. They opened each one and gasped in amazement, as they both took out a gold coin with the head of Adolf Hitler on the front.

"My God – just look at this!" whispered Thomas. "I've never seen anything like this in my life. Imagine what Gus would say if he saw these!"

"Nor me," replied Sally. "Thomas, these must be priceless."

"No wonder Caroline needed an antique dealer. I bet she was selling these to Harold Steel, and he was passing them on to collectors."

"I wonder how many she had to start with? There are eight, here – she could have had dozens."

"I still can't believe it, Sally."

"You know, Thomas, I think Caroline must have left Amy a fortune. Everything she has is very expensive, and her house in Melton must worth a bomb!" Thomas nodded.

"Yes, I have noticed that everything she has is of the best quality." Sally frowned again.

"I wonder why Amy's never had any children? With all her wealth she could have had a big family – I know she likes children."

"I suppose there must be a reason," mused Thomas.

"Let's get the last envelope, Thomas. I want to get out of here, " said Sally earnestly, putting away the coins.

"OK" Thomas opened the last envelope, and took a small pile of papers out, all written in German. "What do you think these are, Sally?" Sally leaned over Thomas's lap, and studied the documents.

"I've no idea." She picked up one and started to translate. "It's a birth certificate – but it's nothing like ours." Sally took the certificate off Thomas and started to read it.

"This one is the birth of Lilli, the next one is her marriage to Hans Muller...the next two are death certificates...Lilli and Hans...and...Franz and Lilli Colberg, the parents...Look, Thomas...this is Fransiska's birth certificate, see...born in Tiergarten, Berlin...

Fransiska Koner...born..10th September 1938...Burggrafenstrasse 31...that's the address...*vater*...that's father...Heinrich Koner...*oberst*...that's his rank...of 10 Panzer Regiment...*evangelisch*...that means protestant...*wohnhaft*...resident...in Burggrafenstrasse 31... Tiergarten...*mutter*...that's mother... Christina Koner...*geborene*...her maiden name...Colberg...*wohnhaft bei eheman*...residing with her husband. Down here is the date her birth was registered...20th September, 1938...and notice this stamp...a Prussian Eagle with a swastika on it's tail."

E 1

Geburtsurkunde

(Standesamt Berlin – Tiergarten Nr. 1483/42)

Heinrich Köner

ist am 1 Marz 1942,

in Berlin, Burggrafenstrasse31, geboren.

Vater: [illegible] avengelisch

wohnhaft . . . Tiergarten.

Mutter: Christina Köner geborene Colberg wonhaft

Burggrafenstrasse 31

Änderungen der Eintragung:

Berlin – Tiergarten, den 10 Marz 1942

Der Standesbeamte

In Vertretung: [signature]

Stand A 27
Mat. 2343 ● Din A 4. 60000. 8. 41

E 1

Geburtsurkunde

(Standesamt Berlin – Tiergarten Nr. 4163/17)

Christina Colberg

ist am 7 Februar 1917

in Berlin Flensburgerstrasse 25 geboren.

Vater: Franz Colberg Lehrer avengelisch wohnhaft Flensburgerstrasse 25 Tiergarten.

Mutter: Lilli Colberg geborene Badel wohnhaft bei ihrem ehemann

Änderungen der Eintragung:

Berlin – Tiergarten, den 15 Februar 1917

Der Standesbeamte

In Vertretung:

Stand A 27
Mat. 2843 ● Din A 4. 60 000. 8. 41

E 1

Geburtsurkunde

(Standesamt Berlin - Tiergarten Nr. 3146/38)

Fransiska Köner

ist am 10 September 1938

in Berlin, Burggrafenstrasse 31, geboren.

Vater: Heinrich Köner Oberst Panzer Regiment 10. avengelisch wohnhafte Burggrafenstrasse 31 Tiergarten.

Mutter: Christina Köner geborene Colberg. wohnhaft bei ihrem Ehemann.

Änderungen der Eintragung:

Berlin - Tiergarten, den 20. September 1938

Der Standesbeamte

In Vertretung:

Stand A 27
Mat. 2843 Din A 4. 60 000. 8. 41

E 1

Geburtsurkunde

(Standesamt Berlin – Tiergarten Nr. 1136/14)

Lilli Colberg

ist am 4 Januar 1914

in Berlin Flensburgerstrasse 25 geboren.

Vater: Franz Colberg. Lehrer. avenglisch.

wohnhaft Flensburgerstrasse 25. Tiegarten

Mutter: Lilli Colberg geborene Badel

wohnhaft bei ihrem eheman.

Änderungen der Eintragung:

Berlin – Tiergarten, den 10 Januaf 1914

Der Standesbeamte

In Vertretung: [signature]

Stand A 27
Mat. 2343 ● Din A 4. 60 000. 8.41

"These are amazing, Sally, what others are there?"

"The next one is Caroline's birth certificate, see...

Christina Colberg..born...Tiergarten....7th February, 1917.... Flensburgerstrasse 25...father..Franz Colberg...der lehrer...school teacher...avenglisch...same address and mother...Lilli Colberg nee Badel. The next certificate is Caroline's marriage to Heinrich Koner..4th April, 1937...register office in Tiergarten...both parents names are on it and the witnesses are Hans and Lilli Muller."

Thomas was fascinated. "I wish I could keep all these," he said wistfully.

Sally laid the certificates on the pile. "Just two left, Thomas, then we must go."

"OK, what's next?" Sally read the next certificate.

"That's funny."

"What is it?"

"This is Heinrich's death certificate – he died in 1940."

"1940! Are you sure?"

"Yes, it's quite clear – look!"

"Of course – it was on that on family tree of Amy's, it just didn't register."

"I wonder who Henry's father was, Thomas?"

"It looks to me as if Caroline had an affair, and Grandfather was illegitimate."

"I bet that's why Amy never told Henry – how sweet of her."

"Yes, it was, but who cares these days? Half the mothers in England aren't married." Sally began to read the last certificate.

"Here we are – Henry's birth certificate! Heinrich Koner.. born 1st March 1942. I can't read the father's name – it looks like someone has tried to rub it out – but the mother is Christine Koner nee Colberg."

"Let me see." Thomas took the certificate and held it up to the light of the table lamp, turning it one way and another. "Bloody Hell!"

"Thomas, what is it," cried Sally, grabbing his arm.

"It's Adolf Hitler – his father was Adolf Hitler!"

"Don't be silly, Thomas, let me see!" Thomas handed the certificate to Sally in a daze. She examined it under the lamp and gasped.

"Thomas, you're right – how awful!"

"I can't believe it," said Thomas in a strangled voice. "It's unthinkable." He shook his head in disbelief.

"No wonder Amy never told anyone – what a terrible shock for her!"

"Poor Amy – and she's had to keep quiet about it all these years – what a nightmare!"

"No wonder she fainted when Fransiska turned up at Henry's – she probably thought she would let the cat out of the bag."

"But she didn't know, Sally. She told Grandfather they had the same father."

"Thank God for that."

"It would certainly explain why Amy was so scared when I turned up. She obviously had no children on purpose – and then I arrived on the scene."

"Poor Amy," said Sally softly," fancy discovering she was the granddaughter of Hitler." Thomas suddenly turned pale.

"God! That means my father was the grandson of Hitler...I'm going to be sick!" Thomas, white–faced, fled to the bathroom, fell to his knees, and vomited into the toilet – he knelt there with his head bent, as the realisation of what he had just discovered, sank in.

Whilst Thomas was in the bathroom, Sally very carefully placed everything back in the box, locked it, and put it back into the safe, and locked that, and lay back the carpet. Realising that Thomas was still in bathroom, she went and knocked the door.

"Are you all right, Thomas?" she called.

"Yes...yes...I'm O.K." Thomas flushed the toilet, and rinsed his mouth and face with cold water. He came out of the bathroom – his face white – his eyes unhappy.

"Let's get out of here, Sally."

"I've put the box away – I'll just draw back the curtains – you hide the keys for Joel." Sally made sure the living room was tidy, and everywhere looked normal.

"Ready?" asked Sally.

"Sally, will you drive? I don't think I could concentrate." He passed her his keys.

"Of course." Thomas set the alarm before they went out. The door locked itself behind them.

When they got outside it was cold and foggy. Sally shivered as she unlocked the car. She settled herself into the driving seat, adjusted it to accommodate her shorter legs, and lowered the driving mirror. Thomas put on the heater and the infra-red lights to guide them through the fog, and set the navigation computer for Oxford.

Sally reversed the car carefully and eased her way along the winding country lanes – the fog was heavy, concealing the hedgerows and the tall graceful trees, which made a green tunnel during the summer when the leafy branches met each other across the road.

By the time they got to the motorway, the fog had started to lift.

"Are you alright," Sally asked the silent Thomas.

"Yes, thanks, Sally. I was just wondering how Andrew Shaw found out about my father."

"Found out?"

"Yes. Remember I told you about Fliss. She said her grandfather was afraid when he knew I'd been born. He must have known."

"But how could he? Why would Amy have told him? I don't suppose even your own father knew."

"Of course, my father wouldn't have known. Amy must have made the discovery months before he died, and I'm quite certain she would never have told him."

"Well, Thomas, we're nearer to solving the mystery of your father than we have ever been."

"Yes, we are. You know, Sally, I would never have guessed what was in Amy's safe if I had lived for ever."

"Neither would I, Thomas. I can still hardly believe it."

"I keep thinking about poor Aunt Amy – frightened of ever having children. I'm not going to have any, either, Sally. I will never bring into this world another descendant of Adolf Hitler!"

They drove on in silence. Sally gripped the steering wheel hard, as her stomach turned over with shock and dismay. Sally adored Thomas, and she had hoped that one day they might marry and have a family. Her dreams were shattered. If she ever married Thomas, she would be childless, like Amy.

Early the next morning Amy was taken down to the theatre. She felt nervous when was she wheeled in on a stretcher, dressed in a white gown and long socks on her feet. Her hand went up nervously to strands of her hair to twist it round her fingers. She gazed at the overhead lights and the bottles and jars lined up behind glass doors. Her consultant, Mr. Jacobs, and his staff were waiting for her wearing green gowns, masks and rubber boots. Mr. Jacobs spoke kindly to her before inserting needles into her arm. Her head swam and her eyes closed.

When Amy woke up she was back in her room, a nurse was taking her blood pressure.

"How are you feeling, Mrs. Brent?"

"A bit sleepy. Am I going to be alright?"

"You're going to be fine, Mrs. Brent, now don't you worry."

"What's happened to me?"

"Mr. Jacobs will be along in a few minutes, and he will tell you everything you want to know."

The nurse smiled, put her instruments in a case, and went out.

Amy lay back on the pillows. She was still wearing her hospital gown and she now also wore a band on her wrist. She looked at it and frowned as Mr. Jacobs walked in. He was tall and slim with neat grey hair, a moustache, and rimless glasses. He was now smartly dressed in a suit and tie. He smiled at Amy, and pointed to the band on her wrist.

"If you have any pain, Mrs. Brent, you just press the dot on the band, and it will release a pain-killer."

"Oh, thank you."

"Now, Mrs. Brent, how are you feeling?"

"I feel alright, I think. What has happened to me?" Mr. Jacobs sat on the chair beside the bed and looked into her anxious blue eyes.

"Mrs. Brent, your fallopian tubes were badly diseased, and I'm afraid we have had to take them away."

"Will I be alright?" she asked nervously.

"You will be fine, Mrs. Brent, there is nothing else wrong with you."

"Thank goodness!" smiled Amy, relieved.

"Mrs. Brent, I have been studying your medical record and I noticed that when you were a teenager you had a burst appendix. I think you will find that this was possibly the cause of your diseased tubes, and that is why you have never had any children."

"What!" gasped Amy.

"I'm afraid so, my dear, there is no way you could have become pregnant without some artificial means."

"You mean, I could never have had children all the time I have been married?" the doctor looked at Amy, a little puzzled.

"I'm sorry, Mrs. Brent, but if we had known earlier we may have been able to help you." Amy was stunned.

"It...it's...alright, Mr. Jacobs," she replied softly. Mr. Jacobs continued.

"You will have only a small scar, Mrs. Brent. The nurse will dress it for you daily. I want you to get plenty of rest when you get home, and no lifting! Your nurse will give you a list of instructions of all the 'do's' and 'don'ts' before you go home, and make an appointment for you to see me in six weeks time for a check-up. Is there anything else you want to ask me?"

"Just one thing," she smiled.

"And what's that?"

"When can I have a cup of tea?" Mr. Jacobs laughed, and wagged his finger.

"Not for another couple of hours I'm afraid."

When the consultant had gone, Amy lay back and closed her eyes. She could hardly believe what she had just been told. She looked up and smiled as her husband walked in, his face full of concern. He went up to her, kissed her and took her hand.

"Are you alright, Darling?"

Amy nodded and told Joel the result of her operation.

"Good God!" exclaimed Joel; "I can't believe it."

"Neither can I. All those years worrying in case I got pregnant, and I couldn't have anyway – it's such a relief. I've always felt guilty about not giving you children, Joel, and not giving my parents any grandchildren, and now I have a reason I can give them." Tears pricked her eyes.

"Don't get upset, Amy, I think it was meant to be, don't you?"

"Yes, you're right, and I do feel as though a great weight has been lifted from my shoulders." Joel stroked her hand.

"Why don't you take up that offer of that job at the local nursery. You can cuddle all those babies now, without feeling guilty." Amy's eyes lit up.

"Oh, Joel, I will. It would be lovely." Joel grinned.

"How about a second honeymoon first?"

"There was nothing wrong with the first one," teased Amy, a blush creeping into her cheeks.

By the afternoon, Amy was washed and fed and wearing a pretty pink nightdress. Henry and Penny had arrived with flowers and a 'get well' card. They kissed their daughter, thankful that she would soon be well. When Amy told her mother what Mr. Jacobs had said, Penny was angry.

"You were on holiday with the school when your appendix burst. It wouldn't have happened if you had been at home!" Amy smiled to herself, and was thankful that her mother would never know the real truth.

A nurse walked in with a huge basket of flowers, which she brought over to Amy.

"I bet these are from Thomas," she said softly. She opened the little card, and inside was written "To Amy, my favourite aunt, get well soon,

Love – Thomas and Sally."

Amy swallowed a lump in her throat. "Oh, Thomas," she thought, "I wish you were my son."

CHAPTER ELEVEN

A GIFT FROM FELICITY – NOVEMBER 2012

Thomas and Sally were deeply distressed after finding Amy's box. He knew it would be hard to face Henry the next time they met and he would have to put on a brave face when he went to Cropwell. He knew that Amy must have gone through the same fear all those years ago. He hoped that Henry's sharp eyes would not notice there was something worrying him.

Even Kal and Gus noticed that Thomas had gone rather quiet and spent much more time with Sally. She was the only person he could talk to, like Amy with Joel they grew close, their terrible secret binding them together.

The days dragged by, and Thomas was trying to get himself back to normal when another shock rocked his life.

One Saturday morning, towards the end of November, Thomas went to collect his post from downstairs, when he found a 'jiffy' bag addressed to him in unknown handwriting, which had been posted in London. He took it into the kitchen, sat at the table, and opened it carefully. Inside were two tapes and a letter. He read it slowly – there was no date or address.

Dear Thomas

I hope you are well. By the time you get this I shall be abroad again. I am enjoying my job very much.

As you may remember, I told you that if I found anything about your father I would let you know. My grandfather, Andrew Shaw, died a few weeks ago, and I have been helping my father clear out his safe, as my grandmother was too upset to do it herself. In the safe I found two tapes (enclosed), in an envelope with the name KENDAL written on it. I have not played the tapes as I have only got a CD player, so I do not know what is on them. I do hope they will be of some use to you.

Best wishes,

Fliss.

PS KAT sends his regards!

Thomas stared at the tapes. His heart was hammering against his ribs and a film of sweat crept over his face. He picked up his mobile, and with a shaking hand dialled Sally's number.

"Sally, it's Thomas."

"What's wrong?" she asked carefully, sensing worry in his voice.

"Have you got a tape recorder?"

"A tape recorder? No, I haven't, but I may be able to borrow one."

"Good girl. Can you get it and come straight round?"

"Thomas, what's happened?"

"I...I'll tell you when you get here."

"OK see you soon."

"Thanks, Sally." Thomas was restless and scared. The tapes must be important for Andrew Shaw to have kept them in his safe. Why weren't they kept at Scotland Yard? Did Andrew Shaw have something on his father that the rest of Special Branch didn't know?

Thomas paced the floor of his flat, running his trembling fingers through his soft, golden hair. What was on those tapes? What was he going to find? He was growing frantic with worry. He needed something to calm him down. He suddenly remembered that he had bought some small cigars for his next visit to Henry. They were in the kitchen drawer. Thomas had never smoked, but the urge for a cigar was overwhelming. He got one out of the packet, and not having a lighter he struggled to light it from the gas hob, and found a saucer to use as an ash tray. He sat at the table and started to smoke the cigar. He felt himself relax.

When Sally arrived the kitchen was full of swirling smoke. She knew there was something terribly wrong.

"Thomas, what's happened?" her brown eyes were full of concern. Thomas showed her the letter from Fliss.

"Read that, Sally." She read the letter slowly, then looked at the tapes and frowned – her lovely face creased with worry.

“I’ve managed to get a tape recorder,” she said quietly, and laid it on the table. They looked at one another.

“I’m scared, Sally.”

“So am I.” They sat at the table and Thomas pushed in the first tape, and with shaking fingers pressed the ‘play’ button. There was a soft hissing and then they heard a man’s deep voice with a Scottish lilt.

“Miss Kendal?”

“Yes.” (Amy sounding nervous)

“Good evening. My name is Andrew Shaw, you are expecting me.”

(Amy) “Yes, of course, please come in.”

Thomas and Sally looked at each other in amazement.

(Amy in a shocked voice) “ Mr. Brown. What are you doing here?”

(Andrew Shaw) “Do we go in here?”

(Amy) “Yes...yes.”

(Joel) “What’s going on?”

(Andrew Shaw) “It’s alright, Mr. Brent. Believe me, Charles Brown is a friend, not an enemy.”

Thomas and Sally looked at each other and frowned.

(Joel sounding angry) “We want an explanation!”

(Andrew Shaw) “Charles, I think you had better explain before we go any further.”

(Charles Brown) “I’m sorry if I have frightened you, Amy, but please believe me when I say that I have been trying to protect you. I really was a friend of your grandmother’s. I first met her in Germany before the war. I was a young soldier stationed over there. I met Christina on a number of occasions, and her sister, Lilli. We weren’t close then, but we were on speaking terms.”

Thomas and Sally listened, puzzled. Who was this Charles Brown who had frightened Amy? The tape continued.

(Charles Brown) “Well, many years later I was in Cropwell, when I bumped into her, and she recognised me. We stopped to talk to each other, and she begged me not to tell anyone that she was from

Germany. She had changed her name to Caroline Kendal. She had her little son, Henry, with her in England and even he didn't know that he had been born over there. Caroline and I often bumped into each other over the years, and she was always grateful that I had kept her secret safe, and she trusted me."

Thomas and Sally sat in silence, enthralled, as the tape played on and Amy's secret was being revealed.

(Charles Brown) "A few years ago she confided in me and asked me to do something for her. She told me that in her cottage she had some documents and photos of her past life. They included a photo of her precious daughter, Fransiska, her sister, Lilli and her husband and parents. She had already arranged for you to have her cottage after her death, and she didn't want you to find them. I told her to destroy them, but she refused, saying she couldn't bear to part with them. We finally agreed that if she died before me, I would come to this cottage as soon as I heard of her death, get the documents from their hiding place and destroy them. She also gave me a key.Well, as you know, she died whilst I was on holiday. I came to the cottage to find them, but found that you had already moved in. You can imagine how shocked I was. I was terrified that you would find the documents before I did. I did not know exactly what they all were, but I did know that your grandmother and Lilli had married Nazi's, and that they were close friends of Hitler, and your grandmother was quite adamant that you were never to see them.

I watched the cottage for a few days as I needed to know what times you went out and came back. One day you threw out a black bag of rubbish. I looked in it and saw that it was full of papers. I took it and searched through it, in case you had thrown them away without realising what they were. Of course they weren't there. The next day I let myself into the cottage and went to the hiding place, which was under the floorboards in the corner of her bedroom. You can imagine my horror when I found they had gone. I was frantic. I searched the cottage from top to bottom, but I still couldn't find them. I'm not a very good burglar, I'm afraid, and that evening you called the police. I was still not sure whether your Gran had already destroyed them or whether you had found them, so I have been following you about, in case you started asking questions. I must say, Amy, you were very careful."

(Amy) "That explains a lot, but why are you here with Mr. Shaw?"

(Andrew Shaw) "We were a little worried about your safety, Amy, may I call you Amy? I have known Charles Brown all my life. He was in the army with my father, and I know you can trust him completely. I asked him to keep an eye on you after your meeting with David Clayton. When we met earlier this evening, he put me in the picture."

(Amy) "Well, what an amazing coincidence. Does Mr. Brown know everything?"

(Andrew Shaw) "He does now, Amy. I wanted someone near you who could be trusted, and he had to know the facts."

(Amy) "You say you knew my Gran's sister – what was she like?"

(Charles Brown) "She was a lovely girl, Amy, fair-haired and blue-eyed and so pretty, just like your Gran. She was full of life and friendly. She and your Gran were very close, and went everywhere together, even their husbands were best friends."

(Amy) "What else can you tell me about them?"

(Charles Brown) "I don't think we have time enough for that now, Amy. I'll visit you again and we can have a chat."

(Andrew Shaw) "Amy, I would like you to tell me all the events that have happened to you since your grandmother died. Please take your time, so that I can digest all the information."

Thomas looked across at Sally and gripped her hand. The two of them sat in silence as they listened to Amy tell her story to the head of Special Branch.

(Amy) "Well, after Gran died, we had the funeral, and a few days later I had a letter from her solicitor, Mr. Hodgekiss, asking me to go and see him. When I got there he told me that Gran had left me everything – her cottage and all her money. My parents had already told me this, so I wasn't surprised, but I did get a shock when he told me that I would have to sign a proviso, which said I was to be discreet with the money and not to give any to my brother, Thomas. I felt awful, but I did want the cottage, and I knew my Gran didn't like my brother, but I never really knew why."

Thomas's hand tightened on Sally's.

(Amy) "Mr. Hodgekiss then gave me a cheque and asked me to sign for it. It was for a huge amount of money, and I was stunned.

When I asked him where she had got so much money, he just said she had made some good investments, and there would be more to come when he had settled her affairs. I felt so guilty about keeping the amount of money from Mum and Dad, that I decided to move into the cottage the next day."

(Andrew Shaw) "Go on, Amy."

(Amy) "Well, I moved in and started cleaning up when I suddenly realised that there were no photos here of my Gran's family – not even one of her dead husband or of her parents. She suddenly became a stranger. I asked Dad, but he didn't know anything about her past, so I started getting curious. I was even more puzzled that evening when Mr. Brown turned up. I was hurt, as we had always been so close, yet she had never mentioned him.

After his visit I decided to start tracing my ancestors, and Joel said he would help me. As my father had only got a short birth certificate I sent off to the local register office for a full one, but they hadn't got it, which was very strange. So I then sent off to a researcher to check the baptisms in the area where he was born, which was in Whitechapel, in London, but that wasn't there either, so I just gave up."

(Andrew Shaw) "When did you find the box?"

(Amy) "It was in the August, whilst my parents were away in Australia. I was digging in the garden, in the flowerbed under the kitchen window, to get out a huge dandelion, when the fork hit something hard. When I looked down I saw the corner of the box. I eventually managed to dig it out – it was like a metal cash box with a handle on top. It was locked and I hadn't a key, Mr. Shaw, when my Gran had her heart attack, she was found in the garden in the pouring rain, which had always puzzled me. I realised that day, that she must have been out in the garden burying that box, and I'm sure that is what killed her. Anyway, I got a screwdriver out of the shed and ran into the kitchen. I was frightened because I thought it was the box that Mr. Brown was after...I finally got it open and found that the contents were all written in German. I was dumbfounded...I rang Joel and he came round with a German dictionary and translated them."

Her voice faltered. "You know what I found."

(Andrew Shaw) "Yes, Amy, and we are truly sorry. It must have been a terrible shock for you. What did you do next?"

(Amy) "Well, we copied all the documents and photos at the bank, the next morning and locked them away, then I got a new box with a key. The following Saturday Joel and I went to the Cropwell Library to try and find out about the coins, but we found that Mr. Brown was following us and I was scared. We eventually managed to give him the slip and went to the library in Melton, but we still couldn't find anything."

(Andrew Shaw) "When did you contact the researcher, Amy?"

(Amy) "The following Monday night. A friend of Joel's found him for us. It was a Mr. Meyer. We asked him to track down Gran's family. I was interested to find out what had happened to Gran's little girl, Fransiska, who she had left in Berlin with her sister, but there was no trace of her. We also asked Mr. Meyer to find the army records of Gran's husband and brother-in-law. A few weeks later we got a letter from Mr. Meyer to say that he had found the deaths of my Gran's parents and her sister, Lilli and Hans, and the birth of Lilli. He couldn't find the death of Fransiska. He also said that he had passed the army record research to another researcher." Her voice faltered.

(Andrew Shaw) "Go on, Amy."

(Amy) "Well...a little while later we got another letter from Mr. Meyer to say that his colleague who was researching the army records had been killed in a 'hit and run'... I was horrified...I thought he had been murdered and it was all my fault...Joel wrote to Mr. Meyer and asked him to stop researching...I wanted to tell the police so Joel and I decided to it would be best to contact Scotland Yard. We didn't know who to speak to and then Joel saw an article in the Daily Telegraph about David Clayton, so we decided to contact him, and we ended up telling him everything."

(Andrew Shaw) "You did quite right, Amy. Now I would like you to tell me about your brother. I understand from David Clayton that your brother isn't quite the saint that everyone thinks he is."

Thomas and Sally looked at each other – their hearts thumping in anticipation.

(Amy) "When we were children Thomas was always very kind to me and we got on well. He used to play with me and read me stories. As we got older I began to realise that he hated anyone who wasn't perfect...he hates black people and people who are fat or ugly or disabled, he...he...used to say that they should have been put down at birth...he also hates criminals and people who hurt children, he says they should be shot...and then there are drug addicts and tramps and people who don't work. He just hates them all..."

(Andrew Shaw) "Has he ever physically harmed any of these people, Amy?"

(Amy) "Oh, no...I don't think he would...but..."

(Andrew Shaw) "But what, Amy?"

(Amy) "Well, he might get someone else to do it for him, perhaps."

(Andrew Shaw) "What makes you say that, Amy?"

(Amy) "I only know of the time he pretended to make friends with a coloured boy in his class at school, who he really hated. I think Thomas framed him for something and the boy got expelled. You see...he arranged it so that someone else got rid of him."

(Andrew Shaw) "I see...Now, Amy, what do you know about your brother's activities at the moment?"

(Amy) "Nothing at all. Thomas is a few years older than me – once he went to university I hardly saw him at all, and when he moved to London and married Joanna, I see him even less. Mr. Shaw, I don't want to get my brother into trouble. I'm only worried about him becoming Prime Minister, because of what he might do, and about him deceiving the public and because he is the grandson of..."

(Andrew Shaw) "Thank you, Amy, you have been very helpful."

There was a slight pause and Thomas and Sally shifted in their seats.

(Andrew Shaw) "This coin is one of a few that Hitler had made when he expected to win the war. There are none on the market, so they must all be in private hands. We will never know whether Hitler gave them to your grandmother as a gift, but as she was given the name of an antique dealer as a contact, I can only assume that he did give them to her with a view of selling them if she, perhaps, fell on hard times. We feel at this stage that the coins belong to you, Amy. I don't know exactly how much they are worth, but I should imagine it would be a very large sum."

(Amy) "Thank you, Mr. Shaw. I'm still not sure what to do with them."

(Andrew Shaw) "Well, you could sell them and make yourself very rich, but then people would start asking you where you found them, or you could leave them locked in the bank for the time being, whilst you make up your mind."

(Amy) "I think I shall do that."

(Andrew Shaw) "Right. This researcher in Berlin who was killed. I have spoken to a contact in Berlin. The hit appears to be genuine. I understand that no–one in Germany knows of your involvement, Amy, but it would not be difficult for some determined person to track down Joel."

(Amy – puzzled) "Mr. Shaw, are you going to investigate the 'hit and run' in case it was murder?"

(Andrew Shaw) "No, Amy, we are not."

(Amy) "But why?"

(Andrew Shaw) "For your safety, Amy. If this man was killed because he was tracing your ancestors, the last thing we want is for that person to know about you. If the killer has got away with murder(if it was murder) he may leave well alone, but if we start poking our noses in and muddying the waters, he may start looking for Joel and you."

(Amy) "You mean, let sleeping dogs lie?"

(Andrew Shaw) "Exactly." There was a pause.

(Andrew Shaw) "Amy, would you be kind enough to make us some coffee before we leave?"

(Amy) "Of course." There followed the sound of a door closing. Amy had left the room.

(Andrew Shaw) "Mr. Brent, I think you and Amy will be quite safe, but you do realise that we cannot give you both twenty-four hours a day protection?"

(Joel) "Of course."

(Andrew Shaw) "If you or Amy ever feel in the slightest danger, or ever need any help, you can call me on any of these numbers and ask for me or my assistant, Peter Malcolm. In the meantime I want you to contact Charles in any emergency and take Amy to his home.

His address is on this piece of paper. You can use Charles's home as a 'safe house' until we can get to you."

(Joel) "Thank you very much."

There followed the sound of rustling paper.

(Andrew Shaw) "Can I ask you a personal question, Mr. Brent?"

(Joel – cautiously) "Yes."

(Andrew Shaw) "Are you and Amy likely to marry?"

(Joel) "I'd love to marry Amy, but I couldn't ask her at the moment, it isn't the right time. Why do you ask?"

(Andrew Shaw) "Because we feel that it may be rather unwise for Amy to have children."

(Joel) "It's OK Mr. Shaw. Amy has already decided that she will never risk having children. She is so afraid of getting pregnant, I'm living like a monk!"

(Andrew Shaw – chuckling) "I've been married many years, laddie, and I almost live like a monk!"

(Charles Brown) "I'm a widower, now, and I live like a monk all the time!"

There was the sound of laughter and a door opening.

(Amy) "What are you lot laughing about?"

(Andrew Shaw) "Just men's talk, Amy."

Thomas and Sally looked at each other and grinned.

There followed some more murmuring and the chink of cups, followed by the rustle of paper.

(Andrew Shaw) "I shall have to ask you both to sign the Official Secrets Act. Please read carefully before signing."

There was a silence.

(Amy) "Goodness – we could go to prison!"

(Andrew Shaw) "I'm sure it won't come to that, Amy. I don't suspect for one minute that you are going to tell anyone."

(Amy) "Of course not!"

There was another silence.

The two listeners sat transfixed.

(Andrew Shaw) "Thank you, both. Charles has already signed one of these, in case you were worried."

There was the sound of movement.

(Andrew Shaw) "Now don't you worry about your brother, Amy. We'll keep a friendly eye on him. If what you say about him is true, we'll just make sure he doesn't get to number 10."

There followed the sound of people moving about and a door opening – a click – and the tape stopped. Thomas and Sally stared at the tape, then looked at each other.

"That was incredible!" gasped Thomas.

"Poor Amy," frowned Sally, "she must have been so scared for such a long time – and that Mr. Brown following her about – how awful!"

"Yes," agreed Thomas, it must have been dreadful for her. I can understand why she looked so afraid when I turned up. It must have brought back all those terrible memories."

"At least we know, now, how Andrew Shaw met Amy. Do you think that researcher was murdered, Thomas?"

"Yes, I'm sure of it – or Andrew Shaw wouldn't have given Joel those emergency numbers or arranged a safe house."

"Maybe that was why they had to sign the Official Secrets Act."

"Yes, plus the fact that they wanted to make sure that no–one was ever to find out that my father was Hitler's grandson, and on his way to becoming Prime Minister." They chatted on.

"I do feel sorry for Amy," went on Sally. "She's gone all these years trying not to get pregnant, only to be told the other day, in hospital, that she could never have had any children anyway."

"She must be so worried in case I ever father a child – how am I going to let her know that I won't?"

"You can't, Thomas." Sally shook her head. "You would have to tell her that we found the box and this tape, and we can't do that."

"That box," went on Thomas wagging his finger at Sally, "we thought she had found it in the house, but Caroline Kendal had buried it in the garden. It was a sheer fluke that Amy found it."

"I wonder why Caroline suddenly decided to bury the box in the garden?"

“I think she may have been feeling unwell, and because Mr. Brown was on holiday she decided to hide it knowing it was close enough to dig up if she wanted it.”

“Of course.” Thomas rewound the tape and took it out of the machine. He looked across at Sally.

“Ready for the next one?” asked Thomas, his inside churning.

Sally nodded, her eyes full of concern. Thomas put in the second tape and pressed the play button, and the tape began to move.

There was a click and they heard a voice – it was a newsreader on the T.V...

“Today Thomas Kendal, the M.P. is seen at Walthamstow Hospital visiting an elderly lady, Edith Jones, who was badly beaten and robbed yesterday by her grandson, who needed money for drugs. Thomas Kendal has offered to pay for Mrs. Jones to have a holiday and her home re–decorated. Mrs. Jones is overjoyed by his kindness. After many such kind deeds Thomas Kendal is now being nick-named ‘Saint Thomas’...”

“Darling, you really are marvellous!”

“That’s my mother!” gasped Thomas.

“Thank you, my sweet.” Thomas stared at Sally.

“That must be my father!” he whispered. The tape continued.

(Joanna) “Don’t you think the old lady should go into a home?”

(Thomas snr.) “Oh, no. She’s normally quite fit for her age, and she is an intelligent woman. She will be quite all right to go home.”

(Joanna) “Have they caught the grandson yet?”

(Thomas snr. sounding angry) “Yes, the little swine’s in custody.”

(Joanna) “Are you going to do anything about him?”

(Thomas snr.) “I certainly am. His days are numbered!”

Thomas and Sally looked at each other in alarm.

(Joanna) “What have you got planned?”

(Thomas snr.) “You know that beautiful old mansion in Walthamstow that’s opening up as a treatment centre for drug-addicts?”

(Joanna) "The one you are angry about?"

(Thomas snr.) "That's the one!" His voice rose in anger. "Angry? I'm furious! The government has spent millions refurbishing a beautiful ancestral home for a bunch of bloody drug addicts. It's a disgrace! The money should have been spent on it for decent people who need help. And what do they do? They spend it on the scum of the earth, and when that old lady's grandson gets there, his next 'fix' will be his last!"

(Joanna) "Good for you, darling!"

(Thomas snr.) "That's not all. I've been asked to go to the opening with that disgusting pop singer, Nico Tolly – God, he's revolting – with his long greasy hair, earrings in every orifice he can find, and his dirty scruffy clothes. He's been bragging to the newspapers that he has been cured of the filthy habit of taking drugs, which is why he has been asked to attend the opening. They even expect me to shake his hand – I hope to God he hasn't got AIDS!"

(Joanna, in a teasing voice) "Never mind, Thomas, you can always wash your hands afterwards."

(Thomas snr. sneering) "What I'd like to do is to get a gun and shoot that piece of shit straight between the eyes."

(Joanna) "Why don't you?"

(Thomas snr.) "No. No. It would be too obvious. Don't worry – I've got something good in store for that bunch of 'junkies'!"

Thomas and Sally looked at each other in horror – and Sally put her hand over Thomas's and held it tightly. They heard the chink of glasses.

(Joanna) "What are you going to do to them all?"

(Thomas snr) "It's best you don't know, darling. The less you know the better."

(Joanna) "What else have you got on the agenda, Thomas?"

(Thomas snr) "I've got a good one lined up for June."

(Joanna – sounding eager) "What is it?"

(Thomas snr) "Well you know Edward and Poppy, who have got all that land up in Yorkshire?"

(Joanna) "Of course."

(Thomas snr) "Well, on 21st June, midsummer day, there are thousands of gypsies going up there for one of their 'get-togethers' and Edward is renting out a couple of his fields. I told him he must be mad, but he said they were paying him a lot of money."

(Joanna) "Stolen money, I expect."

(Thomas snr) "Quite! Now I understand that underneath those fields are some old mine workings, so on that night there is going to be a nice little 'bang' and those fields are going to collapse, taking all those horrible gypsies with them!"

(Joanna) "Thomas, that's marvellous! But what about Edward and Poppy? We don't want them involved or harmed."

(Thomas snr) "Don't worry about them, darling. It so happens that it is Poppy's birthday on 21st June, and as she loves the theatre I have booked seats for us all at the theatre to see 'Miss Saigon'. They will stay the night with us after the show. Edward knows, but I was leaving it as a surprise for you and Poppy."

(Joanna) "Oh, Thomas, that's a wonderful idea. You think of everything!"

The tape wound on silently – the colour had drained out of Thomas's face and he looked ill. Sally's eyes were filling with tears at the sight of his distress.

Eventually the voices resumed.

(Joanna) "Thomas, you are daydreaming again – come along, let's go to bed."

(Thomas snr) "But it's only ten o'clock."

(Joanna) "I said bed, not sleep."

(Thomas snr) "How could a man turn down an offer like that!"

They were both laughing as Thomas switched off the tape in disgust.

Thomas and Sally sat like statues. The silence in the room was only broken by the ominous tapping of rain on the kitchen window.

Thomas's left hand was gripping Sally's hard, his knuckles glowing white. His other hand was supporting his head, his elbow on the table.

Eventually he turned to Sally and spoke to her in a strangled voice.

"My father was a murderer, Sally, a mass murderer, and my mother supported him. He was another Hitler."

Sally stared at Thomas, tears of sadness ran unheeded down her pale face.

"Oh, Thomas, I'm so sorry." He sighed heavily.

"He wasn't killed by mistake, Sally. He was assassinated by Special Branch."

"I think so, too. That's why those tapes were in Andrew Shaw's safe – nobody else knew."

"They must have killed him to save a scandal, but they let my mother get away with it. No wonder she would never go to London, she must have been too scared." Thomas was furious.

"It was certainly a well-kept secret," whispered Sally.

"Yes, and they certainly stopped him getting to number 10!"

"Oh, my God, Amy! What would she say if she knew?" Sally was horrified.

"If Amy hadn't found that box and gone to David Clayton, my father could still be alive and murdering people."

"She's saved a lot of lives without realising it."

"My father must have arranged for all those people in Kendrick House to be poisoned before he died," said Thomas flatly. Sally shuddered and Thomas continued.

"All those newspaper cuttings I got – my father must have been responsible for all those deaths, too, I'm sure of it."

"Thomas, I can hardly believe it," cried Sally.

"Neither can I." Thomas closed his eyes and rubbed a hand nervously along his thigh.

"Sally, I can't believe what's happened to me since I came to Oxford. My life was so smooth and uncomplicated and such fun when I arrived. Then I met Fliss who told me that Special Branch had been watching my father, then I had the first row ever with my mother about my father. Then I met you and discovered my Kendal family who had never been told about me – an aunt who was scared of me. After that you were nearly killed in a 'hit and run', then there was the finding of Amy's box and now this!"

Thomas stifled a sob. "Sally, I don't think I can take much more!"

Sally felt as if her heart were breaking. She got up from her chair and sat on Thomas's lap. She put her arms round his shoulders and he buried his face in her neck, her soft curls touching his cheek. He put his arms round her waist and held her tightly.

"Sally," he mumbled," promise you'll not leave me." Sally laid her cheek against Thomas's fair head.

"I promise," she whispered tearfully.

They sat in silence, clinging to each other.

CHAPTER TWELVE

THOMAS'S REVENGE – DECEMBER 2012

The shock of Thomas's terrible discovery made him feel quite ill, so Sally stayed the weekend at his flat. His life was shattered – the dear father he had always been so proud of was not only the grandson of Adolf Hilter, but a mass murderer. His mother, who was so beautiful, and who he had adored so much as a child, was just as bad.

Thomas eventually developed a terrible migraine. Sally fussed round him like a mother hen, tucked him into bed and drew the curtains. She took his mobile phone to answer his calls and put off all visitors. She then dashed out to the chemist to get him some migraine tablets and got some shopping as the fridge was bare.

When she got back, she went into the bedroom and took Thomas a tablet and a glass of water. Sally looked down and saw the pain in Thomas's eyes.

"Take this, Thomas, and try to sleep," she urged. He swallowed the tablet with a little water and lay down. Sally sat with him until he fell asleep, then went out and quietly shut the door.

To give herself something to do she put away the shopping, and cleaned up the flat. The place was a mess and Thomas's books were lying on the floor along with folders and papers and his mini-computer. When everywhere was clean and tidy, she got herself a sandwich and a drink and sat on the settee and watched the television – the sound turned low.

During the evening Thomas woke up and Sally took him another tablet. He looked up at her and pleaded.

"Don't leave me, Sally."

"I won't leave you, Thomas. Now lie down and get some more sleep." He obeyed her like a child. Sally sat on the side of the bed and gently stroked his head, his hair was soft and silky under her hand.

When she was sure that Thomas was asleep, she crept out of the room, and after making herself a coffee, she made herself comfortable, and slept on the settee.

Sally and Thomas were unaware of the watcher who was standing outside in the shadows.

The following morning Thomas felt a little better, and Sally took him some breakfast in bed. They spent the day sitting on the settee together, talking. They went over all the facts they had discovered and re–read the newspaper cuttings they had got from the library. Thomas shook his head sadly.

"My father was responsible for all these deaths, Sally, I'm sure of it. Look at all these poor, crippled children who were gassed – I'm sure he was behind it – what a monster he was!"

Sally felt uncomfortable, as there was nothing she could say to ease his misery.

"These could be the tip of the iceberg, Sally, how many more people did he have killed?"

"Don't torture yourself, Thomas."

"It's all so unbelievable."

"I know."

Sally stayed with Thomas until the evening.

"I shall have to go now, Thomas."

"Do you have to?"

"Yes. I need a shower and a change of clothes, and my flat mates will wonder where I am, and I don't want them to find out anything, by keep asking me questions."

"Of course, I understand. I'll walk you home."

Thomas walked Sally back to her flat, through cold, dark streets. When they got to her door he put his arms round her, and held her close.

"Sally, I don't know how to thank you for all you've done for me. You really are wonderful."

"So are you," she replied smiling.

Thomas bent his head and kissed her. She put her arms round his waist. They kissed for a long time, a kiss of warmth, love and comfort. When Thomas finally let her go, she went into her flat and Thomas walked back to his own. His head bent, his hands tucked into his jacket pockets, he did not see the dark figure that followed him home, or see him take his mobile phone out of his pocket...

Thomas had a dreadful week. His mind kept wandering and he had a job to concentrate on his studies. When his friends asked him what was wrong, he merely said he had a headache.

Gus and Kal were both worried about him.

"What's wrong with Tom, Kal?"

"I do not know, Gus, but he is most unhappy."

"He's spending a lot of time with Sally, you'd think he would be happy."

"I know. I do not understand it at all."

The following Friday, Kal and Thomas left together after a lecture. It was late afternoon and darkness was falling like a menacing shadow. Kal looked at Thomas and frowned.

"Thomas, my friend, what is wrong?"

"Nothing. I'm, OK."

"Thomas, I can see you are unhappy. I am your friend. Please tell me what is wrong." Thomas sighed.

"Well...I...I've found out something awful about my father, but I can't tell you. I'm sorry."

"That is OK, Thomas, but your father has been dead many years, try and put your troubles behind you."

"Yes, you're right."

"Are you seeing Sally tonight?"

"I'm seeing her later. She wants to wash her hair and do her nails and things."

"Well, I am on my own this evening. Gus is out with one of the girls from his class, another history fanatic, and the girl I have been going out with has had to go home for the weekend to visit her mother in hospital. Why don't we go out for a drink and something to eat. You could phone Sally, and she can meet up with us later." Thomas cheered up a little.

"OK, Let's dump our books and I'll phone her."

Half an hour later the two lads were sitting in the 'Wig and Pen' tucking into scampi and chips and drinking lager.

Meanwhile Sally was in her flat, alone, as her flatmates had still not come in. She felt tired and dispirited and had not slept much all week, worrying about Thomas. It was 5.30. She had decided to have a nice soak in a hot, bubbly bath, wash her hair and manicure her nails. She laid some clean clothes out on her bed, and humming to herself, she made her way into the bathroom, only to find that her bath gel and bottle of shampoo were almost empty. She was furious! Her flatmates had been using them again! Why couldn't they leave her things alone?

Feeling really angry Sally dragged on her jacket, and shoving her purse and keys into the pocket, she stormed out of the flat, slamming the door behind her, and made her way to the supermarket to get some bath gel and shampoo.

The November night was dark, cold and misty. Sally turned up the collar of her jacket. Her head bent, she did not notice the two men, dressed in dark clothes and baseball caps, walking some distance behind her.

When Sally left the supermarket, anxious to get back to her flat, she decided to take a short cut down an alley between two shops. She was still unaware of being followed.

When she was half-way down the alley, Sally heard a noise behind her. She turned and gasped as the two men grabbed her arms and pushed her against a wall. Before she had a chance to scream, one of the men hit her across the face.

"Keep away from Thomas Kendal, you bitch!"

Sally was breathless with shock, when the two men pushed her to the ground and kicked her viciously, before disappearing into the misty darkness.

She lay on the ground in a state of shock, moaning softly. Suddenly the left side of her face began to burn. She put up a hand to her face, and warm, sticky blood began to seep through her fingers. She started to cry, and as she lifted her head, the blood began to run into her eye and mouth. She started to sob, but the tears ran into the cut in her face and made it sting, and burn even more.

Sally struggled to her feet, and half–blinded, staggered down the alley and into the brightly lit street, her face covered in blood. A group of students, passing by, saw her and two of them caught her as she started to fall, feeling sick and faint. One of the girls grabbed some tissues out of her pocket and pressed them onto Sally's face to try and staunch the bleeding. Sally's face had been slashed from her hairline down to her chin, missing her left eye by an inch.

"Get an ambulance!" someone shouted. One of the group pulled a mobile phone off his belt and dialled 999.

Two of the girls comforted Sally. One holding her hand and trying to calm her down, the other trying to wipe away the blood.

"Don't worry, you'll be OK."

"What happened?" asked another.

"I was attacked," whispered Sally, who was in a state of shock and trembling all over. She was frightened and in pain.

An ambulance soon arrived – blue light flashing, followed by a police car. The paramedics jumped out and ran to Sally.

"Any bones broken, love?"

"No," she whispered.

"What happened?"

"I was attacked and kicked."

The two paramedics gently lifted Sally onto a stretcher and eased her into the ambulance. The two policemen asked the students many questions, and they agreed to walk down to the local police station to make statements of what they had seen.

Whilst in the ambulance Sally was being cared for. One of the paramedics gently wiped her face and pressed a sterile cloth onto her wound. The other held Sally's shaking hand. The two paramedics looked at each other wordlessly after seeing the mess of poor Sally's face.

The ambulance soon arrived at the Radcliffe Hospital, and she was wheeled in on a stretcher and taken straight to a small surgery. A nurse came in to her and asked her the usual questions, including her name, address, date of birth and next of kin. She gave Thomas's mobile number as a contact.

A doctor came in and smiled warmly at Sally, and asked her what had happened. She told him and he nodded. He washed his hands and then began to gently examine Sally's white, shocked face.

"Well, young lady, there's no need for you to worry, we'll soon have your pretty face looking like new." Sally tried to smile.

"Now, Sally," he continued after looking at a computer print–out of her medical record, "I'm going to sedate you, as I need you to be calm and still, whilst I stitch your face. You will just feel a tiny prick in your arm, and you will feel drowsy. I shall then give you a couple of injections to freeze your face before I start my needlework. Are you ready?"

"Yes," whispered Sally, who was still in a state of shock. The doctor injected her, and she was soon feeling calm and drowsy. The nurse sat beside her and held her hand.

"Now, Sally, I want you to lie as still as possible, there's a good girl."

The doctor, gently and carefully, with a sophisticated electronic needle, began the slow process of stitching Sally's face.

By 8.30 Thomas and Kal were still sitting in the 'Wig and Pen'. Thomas looked at his watch and frowned.

"Sally's late."

"Why don't you phone her," suggested Kal.

I will." Thomas dialled Sally's number. "It's switched off, that's strange."

"Perhaps it needs charging."

"Yes, you could be right – just like woman to forget," grinned Thomas. He was beginning to feel uneasy, and began slowly rubbing his hands along his thighs, nervously.

His mobile suddenly rang. "That will be her," he exclaimed.

Kal sat and watched the colour drain out of Thomas's face, and a look of anguish crease his handsome features.

"Thank you for letting me know, I'll come at once."

"Thomas, my friend, what is wrong?"

"It's Sally, she's been attacked, she's in the Radcliffe."

Thomas stood up and pushed away the chair.

"I will come with you, yes?"

"Yes, please, Kal, thanks." The two lads left the pub quickly. "We'll get a taxi."

Thomas and Kal walked along George Street, but there was no sign of a taxi.

"Thomas, we can walk, it's not far."

"OK then, come on!" urged Thomas.

They hurried along George Street and turned right into Walton Street towards the Radcliffe Infirmary.

"Thomas," gasped Kal, "what has happened, who was on the phone?"

"It was the hospital. They said that Sally was attacked earlier this evening, and she gave them my mobile number to contact me."

"Is she badly hurt?"

"I don't know, Kal, they didn't say."

"Poor Sally, who would want to hurt her? she is so very nice and kind."

"I know, she's a wonderful girl, and wouldn't hurt a fly. I don't like it, Kal. This is the second time this year that she's been hurt by someone."

"Of course, the car accident in Cropwell."

"She told me, then, that she was sure the driver was trying to kill her, perhaps he's had another go."

"Thomas, we must try and protect her."

"We will, Kal, we will."

Thomas and Kal reached the hospital. It was warm and well–lit inside. They hurried to the reception desk and asked about Sally. The receptionist checked her computer, then turned to Thomas.

"Sally Bennett has just been taken to the ward. She's in the new accident wing – Charlotte Ward – on the first floor. You go down that corridor– the lift is at the end."

"Thank you," replied Thomas," come on Kal!"

They hurried along the corridor and got into the lift. Thomas's inside was churning over with fear and worry over Sally. It was the second time he had been in this situation, and he was scared. They got out of the lift and asked a passing nurse for Sally.

"She's in there," replied the nurse pointing to one of the doors along the corridor. Thomas and Kal walked nervously through the door to see Sally lying in the bed opposite, a nurse checking her blood pressure. They took one look at Sally's face and froze with shock.

"Oh, my God!" whispered Thomas. Suddenly the horror of the past was pushed aside for the horror of the present.

Thomas and Kal looked at each in silence, and moved towards the bed. The nurse spoke to Sally, then moved back.

"Visitors, Sally. Two handsome young men, aren't you the lucky one!"

Thomas sat down beside the bed and took Sally's hand. Kal stood sedately behind his shoulder.

"Hello, Sally," Thomas's voice was soft and gentle. She looked at him dreamily. The left side of her face was badly swollen and bruised. Dried blood was matted in the neat stitches, and in her hair. Thomas was shaking with anger as he realised that someone had almost cut her lovely face in half.

"Hi, Thomas."

"How do you feel?"

"I hurt all over."

"What happened?"

"I was coming back from the shops...I...I...took a short cut through an alley...two men grabbed me and one slashed my face...they pushed me on the floor...and kicked me..."

"Did they say anything?"

"They said something about keep away from Thomas Kendal...you bitch..." Sally's eyes closed.

Thomas and Kal looked at each other in amazement.

"Did I just imagine that?" frowned Thomas.

"No, my friend – Thomas – I am going out to phone Gus. I will wait for you downstairs."

"OK, Kal, you won't go away?"

"Of course not." Kal patted Thomas on the shoulder and left the ward.

"Thomas sat and gazed at Sally. His heart went out to her and his eyes filled with tears. He lay his cheek against her hand – his whole body cloaked in misery.

Kal made his way hastily through the hospital, stood outside and rang Gus on his mobile.

"Gus, it's Kal, can you come to the Radcliffe straight away?"

"What's happened?"

"Sally is here, she's been attacked."

"Bloody Hell, not again! Where's Tom?"

"He's with her now. He's very upset."

"Go and sit in reception, Kal, I'm on my way!"

Kal went back into the hospital, thankful that Gus was coming, he was so strong and capable. He sat on one of the chairs and watched the doorway – waiting for his friend.

"Ten minutes later Gus came striding through the doors, his pony tail swinging. He marched over to Kal and sat down beside him, his face grim. He looked hard at Kal.

"Right – now tell me exactly what's happened!"

Kal told Gus everything. Gus was furious.

"The bastards!" he growled. Kal winced.

"Who could have done such a terrible thing to Sally, Gus, and why?"

"It's obvious," stated Gus vehemently. Kal frowned.

"But who?" Gus tapped Kal on the forehead with a long bony finger.

"Put your brain in gear, Kal. If Sally was attacked in Cropwell and here, she must have been being followed, and Thomas, too, probably, right?" Kal nodded and Gus continued.

"Well, who has already had Tom followed?"

"His mother!" cried Kal.

"Exactly! Now Tom's mother is a snob and a nasty piece of work. She wants our Tom to marry the daughter of one of her mates. Do you honestly think she would sit back and let Tom end up with a nice ordinary girl from a working class family – a girl who has to work as a waitress to earn some pocket money. The girl who told Tom about Henry and Penny? Not on your life!"

"Gus you are right. What are we going to do?"

"First of all we've got to keep an eye on Tom and see if we can spot anyone following him. I'll go and see Sally's two flatmates and ask them to look out for anyone following Sally. When we finally spot someone – we'll sort him out."

"We?" stammered Kal. Gus shook his head.

"Don't worry, Kal. You can be the look-out and I'll do the tough stuff." Kal sighed with relief.

"Do we tell Thomas?"

"Not yet, in case we have got it wrong. We won't tell Sally either, they've enough to worry about. We'll try and sort it first."

"OK," Gus stood up.

"I'm going to Sally's flat now, and I'll bring her back a nightie and things. You wait here, I won't be long."

"OK," Kal nodded and watched his unusual friend walk out of the hospital– head bent – face grim – his hands shoved in the pockets of his jacket.

Gus fascinated Kal. The only child of an elderly professor and his much younger, rather dizzy wife, who had named him Augustus John. He had grown capable and self-sufficient from an early age. Kal sat nervously, his hands between his knees, waiting for his friend's return.

Gus eventually returned, carrying a plastic shopping bag, he marched over to Kal.

"I've got some things for Sally. Let's go!" They made they way up to the ward.

"What did Sally's friends say?"

"They were very upset, but they have agreed to not letting Sally out on her own, and to report to one of us if they think someone is following her."

Thomas had sat quietly beside Sally, watching her with eyes full of sadness and love. Dear Sally, the most wonderful girl he had ever known. Twice she had escaped death – it may be all his fault. Someone did not want Sally to be his partner – it was obvious. She lay with her head tilted to the right to stop any salty tears running into the nine inch wound and making it sting. She drifted in and out of sleep.

When Gus walked into the ward and saw Sally's bruised and butchered face he was shocked to the core. Thomas stood up and the three lads talked quietly together, when a nurse came in.

"I'm afraid you will all have to leave now. You can visit tomorrow after 10 o'clock."

Gus handed the nurse the bag for Sally, and after Thomas had gently kissed Sally, they left.

"When they got outside Thomas rang Sally's parents, who were shocked and upset, and agreed to come up to Oxford for the weekend to see their daughter.

The three friends walked to the nearest bar, where Gus bought them all a stiff drink. They sat in a corner and talked earnestly together until closing time. When they left the bar Gus and Kal insisted that Thomas go back to their flat for the night, as he was too shocked and depressed to be left alone.

They all spent a disturbed and restless night.

When Sally woke the next morning she felt a little better, although her face and her body were still sore. She had had a full body scan the evening before, and was thankful, once again, that she had no serious internal injuries.

She felt weak and dirty after her ordeal and was grateful when two nurses eased her into a warm bath. She sponged her body carefully, looking at the bruises that were forming on her battered limbs. One of the nurses gently washed her hair, removing dried blood, dirt and gravel, and bathed her face. They helped her into a clean cotton T-shirt type nightdress with a big rabbit on the front, and helped her into bed, and brought her a light breakfast.

It was Saturday, and Sally was inundated with visitors who brought her flowers, chocolates and get–well cards. Thomas spent the day with her, and Gus and Kal called in. Her two flat mates arrived and many students from her class and the choir, and a couple of her tutors. Molly and Richard also arrived during the morning and were deeply upset at the sight of their beloved daughter, who looked unrecognisable with most of her face black and blue and swollen and her left eye almost closed.

A policewoman also came to see Sally with a plainclothes detective, who took photographs of Sally's injuries, and told her how to claim for criminal injuries. The policewoman who was tall and well–made and very efficient was kind to Sally. She asked her many questions about her attackers, but it had been too dark and they had been dressed in dark clothes. They had both been slightly taller than her, and the one who spoke had a London accent. Everything had happened too quickly for her notice anything else. Sally told the policewoman that she would be unable to identify them if she met them again. The policewoman wrote down a statement, and Sally signed it.

The Press, who also took her photograph, which was to be put in the local paper with an article asking members of the public if they had seen the two men running away, visited Sally.

Sally spent the weekend in hospital, and was allowed to go back to her flat on the Monday morning. Her flatmates, Judy and Jo, had promised Thomas that they would not let her out on her own. Thomas, Gus and Kal agreed to be on call any time that Sally needed a bodyguard. They protected her well.

Gus was feeling uneasy about Kal. He knew that Joanna Kendal hated black people, and was hoping that she wouldn't send her 'bully boys' after him, too. He kept a watchful eye on his rather timid friend.

November had slipped, unnoticed, into December. The shops were full of Christmas decorations, and the streets were busy.

By the following Friday Gus and Kal were convinced they had spotted someone following Thomas. He was a slim, dark youth wearing jeans and a black leather jacket. Gus was ready for action, but Kal was scared.

On the Friday evening they watched him follow Thomas to Sally's flat. Gus nudged Kal.

"Come on, let's go for a drink, and then we'll wait for that little bastard when he follows Tom home. It will be quite late by then. We'll grab him and take him down to the canal."

"You're not going to drown him are you, Gus?"

"Well, not until after he's talked," teased Gus, grinning and shoving his glasses along his bony nose.

"Gus, you joke with me."

By 11 o'clock Gus and Kal, dressed warmly in dark clothes, were hiding amongst the trees opposite Thomas's flat, waiting for their quarry. Thomas eventually came home and let himself into his flat. The street was quiet – the night dark. The moon was hiding behind dark scurrying clouds. The watcher walked past the trees – took out his mobile phone and headed for the end of the street towards the canal.

"Perfect!" thought Gus.

He nudged Kal. "As soon as he's finished on the phone..." Seconds later Gus and Kal crept up behind the young man, and before Kal had time to think, Gus had his arm hooked round the man's throat. He struggled, but Gus was extremely strong, and dragged him to the edge of the canal.

"Right, Pal!" snapped Gus. "Why are you following my friend?"

"F*** off!" sneered the man.

In one swift movement Gus had the man on the ground. He sat across his chest, pinning his arms. Gus grabbed the man's hair and pulled it until his eyes watered.

"Right – I'll ask you again. Why are you following my friend?"

"None of your effing business, mate!" Gus was getting angry. He grabbed the collar of the man's jacket, eased his body up over the man's chest, and pushed his head into the freezing waters of the Oxford canal. After a few seconds of fierce struggling, Gus lifted the man's head out of the water. He was choking and spluttering, his teeth chattering.

"I'll ask you again..."

"OK. OK" spluttered the man, trying to put up his hands.

"Well?" demanded Gus.

"I'm just being paid to follow him."

"That's not enough. Who are you working for?"

"Abercrombie Detective Agency,"

"Where's that?"

"London."

"Why did you attack my friend's girl friend?"

"That wasn't me! I swear to God! I only follow people – I don't do the heavy stuff." His teeth began chattering again – his face and hair were wet and covered in slime.

"Who's paying Abercrombie to have my friend followed?"

The man was silent.

"If you don't tell me, you pathetic little prick, I'll drown you." Gus's voice was menacing. The man was now afraid.

"The mother," he stammered, "the boy's mother."

"I thought so," murmured Gus with satisfaction.

"That wasn't so bad, was it?" The man shook his head.

"You go back to Mr. Abercrombie, and tell him to lay off his watchdogs. Understood?" The man nodded.

Gus got up, slowly, picked up the man by his trouser belt and jacket collar, and threw him into the canal.

Gus and Kal ran off leaving the man splashing and flailing in the freezing, dark, dirty water.

"Gus, what if he can't swim?"

"Tough!" was the firm reply.

"Do you think he attacked Sally?"

"No, Sally's attacker had a London accent and he didn't."

"Do you think we should go to the police?"

"No, They won't be able to do anything."

Minutes later Gus and Kal were sitting in Thomas's flat. Kal sat primly on the settee, his shaking hands tucked between his knees. Gus, who was not one for beating about the bush, told Thomas everything.

Thomas listened in silence, then slowly nodded his head, and looked at Gus. "I should have guessed," he said quietly.

"What are you going to do, Tom?" asked Gus, raising his eyebrows. Thomas, his face looking haggard and drawn, his eyes narrowed, gave Gus a grim smile.

"I've got something on my mother you wouldn't believe. When I go and see her in the morning – she'll be finished."

Thomas set off for Westlake Manor early the next morning. He hated his mother so much he wanted to see her in Hell. He drove up to his ancestral home, which looked so beautiful, set amongst the trees, under the glow of a wintry sun.

He parked his car outside the main doors, climbed the steps, and let himself into the magnificent hall with it's large elaborate staircase and paintings of his ancestors lining the walls. He came face to face with Emma.

"Where's Mother?" he asked rather curtly.

"In the drawing room, dear, is there something wrong?"

"Please don't disturb us," he stated firmly.

He walked into the drawing room and slammed the door. His mother, who was looking out of a window, turned in alarm. She looked beautiful, as always.

"Thomas, darling, what a surprise!" She walked towards him, her jewelled hands outstretched.

"Don't 'darling' me, you murdering bitch!"

"Thomas!" gasped Joanna. "Whatever is wrong?"

"You know very well what's wrong. You've been having me and Sally followed, and you've paid to have her attacked twice!"

"I don't know what you are talking about!" she stormed.

"Oh yes you do. You had her almost killed in Cropwell, when she was hit by a car, and now this!" He wrenched a folded newspaper out of his jacket, with a picture of Sally's battered face splashed across the front page. He shook it out in front of his mother's face. She stepped back in horror, and glared at her son.

"How dare you accuse me of such a thing!" she yelled. "If you continue to speak to me in this manner, I shall cut you out of my will!"

"I don't think so, Mother." Thomas's voice was like steel – cold and hard. "You try a trick like that and I'll see that you spend the rest of your life in prison!"

"What on earth are you talking about?" babbled Joanna.

Thomas moved close to his mother and slid a hand round her throat.

"I know all about the dirty tricks you and my father were up to before he was killed."

"W...what...on earth do you mean?" Joanna began to turn pale. Thomas mimicked his mother's voice and said...

"Oh, Thomas, darling, how wonderful you are. One little bang and all those nasty gypsies will fall into the hole..."

Joanna's legs almost gave way beneath her.

"How...how..?" she gasped.

"How did I find out? Wouldn't you like to know!"

Thomas's hand slipped from his mother's throat and down to her chest and pushed her into the nearest armchair. She sank into it, weak and frightened. Thomas leaned over his mother, resting his hands either side of her on the arms of the chair. He looked hard into his mother's blue, staring eyes.

"You and my father were a couple of murderers – and don't think he was killed by accident – he wasn't – he was assassinated by Special Branch. They must have let you off – but I won't! If you ever let anything else happen to Sally or anyone else I care about, I'll ruin you. If she so much as trips over a matchstick, I'll go to the newspapers and to the police with all the evidence I've got, and you will be locked away for ever. Is that clear?"

"Yes, Thomas," she whispered hoarsely. He snatched the dainty mobile phone from her belt.

"Now phone your Mr. Abercrombie, and tell him to lay off his watchdogs – NOW!"

"Yes, Thomas." Her voice and hands were trembling as she dialled the number.

"He...he's out..." she stammered.

"Then leave a message!"

"Mr. Abercrombie...this is Joanna Kendal speaking...could you please cease the surveillance on my son and send me your bill...thank you."

"That's better." Thomas looked at his mother with eyes full of hate. "I never want to see you again – as long as I live."

He stood up, turned and walked out of the room, and out of his mother's life. He left the house, climbed into his car and sped away.

When Thomas had gone, Joanna sat in the armchair, a shivering wreck. How had Thomas found out? Had the Special Branch bugged their house? How had they ever discovered what her husband had been doing? She was terrified.

With trembling hands she picked up her mobile and dialled the airport. She booked herself on to the next available flight to Spain, which left in four hours time. She stood up with legs like jelly, and made her way to the hall. She wearily climbed the magnificent staircase, went to her bedroom, and started to pack.

After driving a couple of miles, Thomas suddenly started to shake. He pulled into a lay-by surrounded by trees, and stopped the car. The shock of what he had just done had suddenly hit him. He sat back in his seat, and pulled out of his pocket a packet of small cigars. He lit one and opened the car window to clear away the smoke. He sat puffing away quietly, until his body had calmed down. After taking a few deep breaths he fired the engine and drove carefully back to Oxford and Sally.

When Thomas got back he went straight to Sally and told her everything. She was dumfounded. She looked at Thomas.

"I don't know how two such evil people could produce such a nice person as you, Thomas. You are so kind and thoughtful and good."

"Thank you, Sally."

"You must take after your grandparents – Henry and Penny are lovely people, and your other grandparents sound lovely, too. I'd love to meet them."

"You will, one day." Sally was to meet them sooner than she expected.

When Joanna had packed she went to say goodbye to her parents, and the chauffeur drove her to the airport.

Emma had tried to listen to the row between her daughter and grandson, but her hearing was not too good. She went into the drawing room and looked round. She spotted the newspaper lying on the floor, and picked it up. She saw the picture of Sally and read the article. She frowned – this was surely Thomas's girlfriend – the girl who lived next–door to Henry and Penny. Emma's mouth was grim. She had a good idea what the trouble was, now. Poor Thomas! Emma hid the newspaper and went to talk to her husband.

Thomas and Sally spent the day at Sally's flat. Her face was still a mess and she didn't want to go out. She still felt traumatised after her attack.

During that afternoon Thomas had a call on his mobile. It was Emma.

"Thomas, dear, I though you should know that your mother has gone to live in Spain – in our villa at La Manga Club. She won't be coming back."

"I see," replied Thomas, carefully.

"Now, Thomas," went on Emma, "your grandfather and I are alone now, and we were wondering if you and the Kendals and Sally and her parents would all like to come to Westlake Manor for Christmas and New Year. We'd love you all to come, and it would be such fun!"

Thomas's eyes lit up.

"Grandmother, that's the best offer I've had all year! It's a wonderful idea. I'll contact everyone and get back to you."

"Thank you dear, bye for now."

Thomas turned to Sally and told her about Emma's invitation.

"Oh, Thomas, how lovely! I'd love to meet them and see your wonderful home." Thomas picked up his mobile and started making calls.

It was Christmas Eve, and the country was white with frost, sparkling in the rising sun.

The Kendals and the Bennett's finished packing and set off together in a hired mini–bus to Westlake Manor. Joel and Thomas taking it in turns to drive.

They were happy and excited. Penny was telling Molly and Richard all about the Westlake's ancestral mansion and the beauty of the Lake District.

When they arrived, Westlake Manor looked warm and welcoming, with lights blazing from the many windows. Emma and Marcus were thrilled when their guests arrived – they loved entertaining. The butler took luggage up to all the rooms whilst everyone settled in.

They all had a wonderful Christmas and New Year. There was a twelve foot Christmas tree in the drawing room, with gifts for everyone sprawled underneath – all beautifully wrapped. Meals were taken in the enormous dining room, and everyone was waited on hand and foot. Emma was always kind to her staff and they all loved her devotedly.

Emma and Marcus took their guests on walks and introduced them to their friends. On New Years Eve they had a huge party with dozens of guests of all ages, and a live band. Even the staff was invited, and Thomas introduced Sally to Tim, his backward friend, the son of the gardener, who worshipped Thomas. Sally was deeply touched by Thomas's kindness to him.

After the church bells had rung in the New Year and they had all sung 'Auld lang syne', Thomas and Sally put on their coats and stepped outside.

"It's so beautiful here, Thomas," she breathed.

He looked at Sally with smiling eyes. She looked so lovely. Her face was healing well, and cleverly covered by make–up and her soft brown curls which tickled her chin and neck. Her beautiful eyes were shining, her lovely mouth in a wide smile.

"It will all be mine one day."

"You are very lucky."

"Perhaps you would like to share it with me one day, as my wife?"

"I would like that very much, Thomas, but if you only had a tent to offer me – I would still love you."

CHAPTER THIRTEEN

EMMA'S SECRET - MARCH 2013

A New Year had begun and Thomas and Sally decided to try and put the past behind them, and look forward to the future.

Thomas wanted Sally to move into his flat, but she was worried that her flat mates would let her room, needing her share of the rent, and she would then have to find new accommodation when Thomas left Oxford in the summer. In the end they agreed that she would stay in her flat during the week, but spend her weekends with Thomas. They both took care not to get Sally pregnant.

Thomas loved the weekends. Sally was so good to have around. She was so cheerful and easy-going and comfortable to be with, and she would sing happily to herself as she cleaned the flat and cooked meals, and she was warm and loving in bed.

Gus and Kal now had steady girlfriends. Gus was going out with Kate, a rather intense girl with short, dark spiky hair, and Kal with a petite blonde called Elizabeth. The six of them got on well and saw a lot of each other.

Thomas's life was just settling nicely, when life had another surprise in store for him.

It was in the middle of March when Thomas got a phone call from Marcus.

"Ah, Thomas, by boy, I'm sorry to bother you."

"That's alright, Grandfather, how are you?"

"I'm fine thank you, Thomas, but I'm afraid your grandmother is not well. She's had a slight heart attack."

"Is she going to be alright?" asked Thomas, his heart sinking.

"Yes she is. She's coming out of hospital today, and I've employed a nurse to look after her. Now, Thomas, your grandmother would like to see you, could you come down this weekend?"

"Of course I can."

"Do bring your young lady along, Thomas, she would be most welcome."

"She won't be able to I'm afraid. There's a 'do' on at the Cathedral on Saturday night and she is singing in the choir."

They chatted for a while longer before ringing off. Thomas sighed. He thought his troubles were over, and now his dear grandmother was ill. Bad news seemed to go on for ever!

On the Saturday morning Thomas set off for Westlake Manor. It was a beautiful spring day. Gardens were filled with daffodils and tulips, the trees full of blossom and the fields full of dancing lambs chasing each other. The day was warm and sunny and it was a pleasure to be driving along the country lanes bursting with greenery.

Thomas arrived at Westlake Manor, and was greeted warmly by Marcus.

"Thank you for coming, Thomas."

"How is she?"

"She's fine, just rather tired."

"Where is she?"

"Up in her room. She's looking forward to seeing you." Thomas bounded up the staircase, dumped his overnight bag in his bedroom, and went and tapped on his grandmother's door.

"Come in, Thomas." He entered her room and walked over to the bed. Emma was lying propped up against the pillows, looking rather pale, her blue eyes tired. Thomas bent to kiss her cheek, and as always, she smelled of expensive perfume.

"Hello, Grandmother. What have you been up to?" he teased.

"Nothing much, dear, just had a little scare. Now come and sit beside me." She patted the chair next to the bed and Thomas sat down.

"Now, Thomas, there are things I want to discuss with you before I die."

"Grandmother, please..."

"Thomas – it's no good pretending it won't happen. You know, Thomas, it's a funny thing, but as we go through life we don't actually feel any older, although we may look it! We carry on as if we are going to live for ever, but this heart attack has made me realise that my life is drawing to it's close."

"Grandmother, please don't," begged Thomas. "You could live for many years yet."

"I know that, Thomas, but I am almost seventy already. Now, first of all I want to discuss mine and your grandfather's wills. When we die we are going to leave Westlake Manor to you."

"But what about Mother?"

"Your mother is not coming back here, Thomas, so she is not having it. We are leaving her the villa in Spain, where she is living now, and we shall leave her enough money to live in comfort. Everything else will come to you." Thomas was so surprised he hardly knew what to say.

"Thank you...I don't know what else to say."

"There's no need, dear. I know you will take great care of this lovely home of ours, and I know you won't sell the land for shops or houses to be built, and I know you won't turn out the tenants from their cottages and put your friends in. I know your mother might, but I trust you, Thomas."

"You have my word, Grandmother."

"I know that, dear." She hesitated for a moment. "Thomas, there is just one other little thing..."

"Yes."

"I'm going to tell you a little secret – no one knows but Marcus."

"Go on."

"Well I know you have always been proud of your ancestors, and I know how happy you were when you found your Kendal family, as you have so few relatives – but I'm afraid your ancestral line has a bit of a bend in it!" Thomas laughed.

"What on earth are you trying to say?" Emma looked Thomas straight in the eye."

"I was adopted, Thomas."

"Adopted?"

"Yes. I was the illegitimate daughter of the maid!"

Thomas threw back his head and laughed.

"You're pulling my leg!"

"No, dear, it's quite true."

"I think you had better explain, Grandmother!" Thomas was still chuckling, when Emma continued.

"My real mother's name was Amelia. She was born into a family of schoolteachers, and she came here to learn the language."

"Where was she from?"

"She came from Berlin in Germany – just before the war."

Thomas felt an icy hand grip his heart.

"Berlin?"

"Oh, yes. Well, as I say, she came over here as a maid to improve her English, and she fell in love with my father's younger brother, Charles. Charles was a very handsome, dashing young pilot in the RAF. Amelia and Charles wanted to marry, but she was afraid of what her family would say. She knew they would not approve of her marrying an Englishman. The war began and Amelia refused to go home. Well, eventually the inevitable happened. She got pregnant, and Charles was killed. My parents agreed to look after Amelia and the baby, as they were childless and the baby would be their niece or nephew.

Well, the day after I was born, Amelia died, and I was left an orphan, so my parents adopted me. So you see, Thomas, my parents weren't my real mother and father, they were my aunt and uncle."

"Well, I'll be damned!" exclaimed Thomas.

"Now, Thomas," went on Emma,"I have a few things that belonged to my real mother, and I want you to have them. In the bottom right–hand drawer of my dressing–table you will find an envelope with 'AMELIA' written on it."

Thomas went over and fetched it, his stomach churning.

"You can take it with you to your room and have a look at the contents, whilst I have a little sleep."

Thomas kissed Emma and went off to his room with the envelope. He sat on the bed, tipped out the contents, and slowly looked through them.

On the top were two photographs. One was a wedding picture, and the other one was of a man and a woman sitting in an open

topped car. The woman was wearing a suit and hat and the man the uniform of a German soldier. On the back was written *Anna und Klaus*. Thomas frowned and a shiver ran down his spine.

The next item was a photo of a dog, a setter, followed by a small document written in German, which he couldn't understand at all. Next were two letters. Thomas opened them out, but all he could understand was that they were to Amelia from Anna – was this the girl in the photo? Thomas was wishing that Sally was with him. He would have to wait until he got back to Oxford for her to translate them.

Thomas unfolded the last document and recognised it straight away. It was a Berlin birth certificate – exactly like the ones in Amy's box. He stared at it intently. It was Amelia's birth certificate. Her name was Amelia Colberg – born 7th October, 1918. Her parents were Franz Colberg and Lilli Badel. Thomas's heart started to thump. These names were familiar! He picked up his mobile and rang Sally.

"Sally's it's Thomas, you'll never guess what has happened!"

"Thomas, what is it?" Thomas told Sally about Emma's secret and the documents.

"Have you still got that chart we copied from Amy's box?"

"I'll get it, hold on!" Sally was soon back with the chart in her hand. "I've got it!"

"Right. Now have a look for Colberg and see if this Amelia fits in!" Thomas waited in suspense for Sally to answer.

"Thomas, you are not going to believe this!"

"What is it?"

"Amelia Colberg was the sister of Christina Colberg!"

"Sister! Are you sure?"

"Yes. And you know what that means?"

"No."

"It means that your grandmother, Emma and your grandfather, Henry Kendal are cousins!"

"Cousins! Are you sure?"

"Yes, their mothers were sisters."

"I can't believe it," gasped Thomas.

E 1

Geburtsurkunde

(Standesamt Berlin - Tiergarten Nr. 7234 / 18)

Amelia Colberg

ist am 7 Oktober 1918

in Berlin Flensburgerstrasse 25, geboren.

Vater: Franz Colberg Lehrer avenglisch

wohnhaft Flensburgerstrasse 25 Tiergarten

Mutter: Lilli Colberg geborene Badal

wohnhaft bei ihrem eheman

Änderungen der Eintragung:

Berlin - Tiergarten, den 16 Oktober 1918

Der Standesbeamte

In Vertretung:

(Siegel)

Stand A 27
Mat. 2343 Din A 4. 60 000. 8. 41

B. HILZ Nachf.

Postscheckkonto: München 24022.
Fernsprecher: Prien 151.

Prien, den 20. November 1936

Eideesstattliche Erklärung.

Es wird hiermit eidesstattlich erklärt, dass die Jrisch Setter Hündin

„ Fruh v.d. Klause " in die Satmmrolle bezw. beim Zuchtbuchamt der Fachschaft für engl. Vorstehhunde eingetrageh ist.

Die Ahnentafel des Wurfbruders Falk v.d. Klause liegt hier vor und trägt die Nummer 6341 & ist unter den 15.2.1937 eingetragen.

Als Züchter ist Herr Hubert Schröffel München Agnesstrasse 64/0 vorgetrageh.

Vater : Ilor LydiaPSSTB 5238
Mutter: Angara v. Hapichtshof PSSST 4676

Für die Richtigkeit der Abschrift :

Prien, 20. November 1936

St. Ochs

I. Bügermeister Prien

“Nor me. What an amazing coincidence! Thomas have your grandparents got a FAX machine? You could fax me the documents.”

“I don’t want to risk it, Sally. I would have to fax them to Keble, and I don’t want anyone to see them.”

“OK. I’ll just have to wait until tomorrow. What time will you be back?”

“Late afternoon. I can’t really leave here any earlier.”

“OK. I’ll be waiting at your flat.”

“Good luck for tonight. I’m sorry I can’t be there.”

“Don’t worry, it can’t be helped. See you tomorrow.”

“Bye, Sally.” Thomas put down his phone, and stared again at the documents – shaking his head in disbelief.

Thomas spent a pleasant weekend with his grandparents at Westlake Manor. When he asked Emma if he could show the documents to Sally, for her translate, she had said.

“Of course, dear. It’s no big secret now, anyway.”

Before lunch Thomas went to visit Tim and his parents, who were all pleased to see him. Thomas enjoyed a Sunday lunch with Marcus, as Emma had hers in bed. He later sat with her until she fell asleep. He left shortly afterwards, promising to visit again soon, with Sally.

Thomas was impatient to get back to Oxford. He arrived at his flat at 5 o’clock to find Sally waiting for him anxiously. They made their way into the living room and Thomas showed her the documents and photos.

She looked at the birth certificate of Amelia first, and compared it with the chart.

Yes, Amelia was definitely Christina’s sister, they had the same parents, and I’m sure the address is the same, too.” She looked at the photo of the dog, and the attached document.

“This is a pedigree, Thomas. Perhaps this was her pet dog. She began to translate...sworn declaration...it is here sworn...that the Irish setter bitch Fruh v.d. Klause has been entered into the book of lineage...the litter is kept here...and the breeder is a Mr. Hubert. It the gives the names of the dogs parents and dates. Let me see the letters.”

Sally read through the letters, slowly.

"What do they say?" urged Thomas

"I think," replied Sally slowly," that this Anna is another sister – yes she is – look at the end of this letter – 'your loving sister, Anna' and this second letter is addressed to Amelia, my little sister."

"That means that Caroline Kendal had three sisters, not one!" exclaimed Thomas.

"That's right."

"What's in the letters, Sally?"

"The first one is dated 1st June, 1938 and says – Dear Amelia, I hope you are well, and have settled in England. We hope you will not stay too long, as they say that we may soon be at war. Klaus and I were sad that you could not be at our wedding, but I have sent you two photos of us. Mother and father are well and Lilli too. Christina is expecting her first baby soon. We are all excited. Please write soon and tell us about your employers – are they kind to you? We hope so. Please come home soon. Your loving sister, Anna."

"That's incredible – she mentions Christina and Lilli – there can be no mistake – my two sets of grandparents are related."

"Yes, and look at all these wedding guests – they could be your relations! Christina must have been expecting Fransiska. Look, she was born on 10th September, 1938."

"That's right. What does the second letter say, Sally?"

Sally read it through quickly, then translated it for Thomas.

"This one is dated in April, 1943 – some years later. It starts– Amelia, my little sister – I hope this letter reaches you safely – it has had to be sent through agents as you know I cannot post it. We are very worried about you – why have you not come home? Have you still got the same boyfriend? You know our parents would not have approved if they were still alive. Since my last letter I have had a son, Klaus, named after his father, of course. He is very beautiful. I wish you could see him. Christina is away on a secret mission, and has taken Hienrich with her. Fransiska is staying with Lilli and Hans – they adore her. Lilli still has no children of her own – she is very sad. Please try and contact us soon – we have not heard from you for some time. Please come home soon – we will find a way. Love, Anna."

"That's amazing – everything seems to fit perfectly."

"It certainly does. You know, Thomas, there's a big gap between these letters – I wonder what happened to the others?"

"Perhaps they were thrown away – or they may be hidden somewhere." suggested Thomas.

"Thomas, those letters in Amy's box – I'm sure there was a reference to Anna and Amelia." Thomas suddenly looked thoughtful.

"I would love to show all this to Amy."

"That would be risky, Thomas."

"I know. I would have to tell her that I found the box. She might be really angry."

"Come on, Thomas, let's add these names on to this chart." she frowned. "It might look a mess. I'll do a new one."

Thomas fetched Sally a fresh piece of paper, and in her neat handwriting she wrote out a new chart, adding Christina's two sisters and Emma Westlake on to the Kendal family tree.

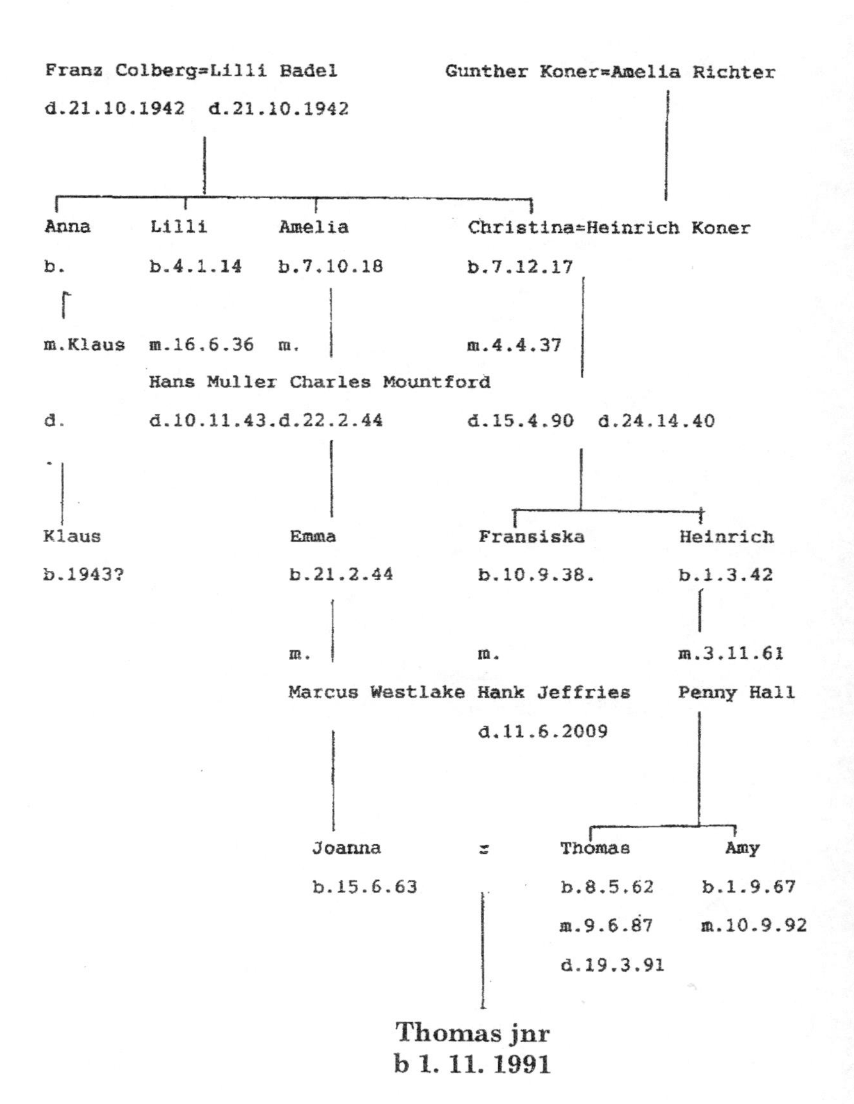

Franz Colberg=Lilli Badel
d.21.10.1942 d.21.10.1942
Gunther Koner=Amelia Richter
Anna
b.
m.Klaus
d.
Lilli
b.4.1.14
m.16.6.36
Hans Muller
d.10.11.43.
Amelia
b.7.10.18
m.
Charles Mountford
d.22.2.44
Christina=Heinrich Koner
b.7.12.17
m.4.4.37
d.15.4.90 d.24.14.40
Klaus
b.1943?
Emma
b.21.2.44
m.
Marcus Westlake
Fransiska
b.10.9.38.
m.
Hank Jeffries
d.11.6.2009
Heinrich
b.1.3.42
m.3.11.61
Penny Hall
Joanna
b.15.6.63
=
Thomas
b.8.5.62
m.9.6.87
d.19.3.91
Amy
b.1.9.67
m.10.9.92
Thomas jnr
b 1. 11. 1991

CHAPTER FOURTEEN

A NEW LIFE FOR THOMAS – 2013

Thomas was restless. He still couldn't forget the dreadful tape of his parents plotting all those murders, and he badly wanted to share Emma's secret with Amy.

"What shall I do, Sally?"

"It's up to you, Thomas. Do what you feel is right." Thomas was thoughtful.

"I know what I'll do – I'll speak to Joel."

"That's a good idea, Thomas. Joel is so good and sensible, and already knows about Amy's box. He would be the perfect person to talk to."

"What shall I do about the tapes?"

"Well... I don't think I would let him hear the first one, he might be embarrassed and annoyed to find that Special Branch taped his conversation at the cottage."

"Yes, you're right, but I will play him the second one, and leave it up to him whether we should tell Amy."

"Good idea."

Thomas rang Joel at the bank in Melton Mowbray.

"Joel, it's Thomas."

"Hello, Thomas. What can I do for you?"

"I...I...need to talk to you...alone."

"What's it all about, Thomas?"

"My father."

"I see...very well. Can you come down to the bank on Saturday morning, about ten? I often call in here on a Saturday morning, so Amy won't be suspicious. Do you know where the bank is?"

"Yes, I do, and thanks, Joel."

"OK, Thomas, see you on Saturday." Joel was deep in thought as he put down the phone.

At 10 o'clock on the following Saturday morning, Thomas arrived at Martin's bank. Joel, who looked extremely smart and efficient, was waiting for him, and ushered him into his office. Thomas was feeling nervous as he sat opposite Joel – the desk between them.

"No-one can hear us, can they?"

"No," replied Joel, who pressed the 'Do Not Disturb' button on his desk.

"Right, Thomas, what's this all about?" Thomas clutched the brief-case that lay on his lap, and began to tell Joel of the events that had taken over his life.

"When I arrived in Oxford I was so happy and carefree, and so proud of my dead father – I wanted to be just like him." Joel nodded, his eyes watchful.

"Well, towards the end of my first year I got friendly with a girl called Fliss, she was the granddaughter of a man called Andrew Shaw, who was the head of Special Branch when my father was an M.P." Joel raised his eyebrows, trying to conceal his alarm.

"On our last night together we got a bit drunk, and she told me that Special Branch had been watching my father. I begged her to tell me what she knew, but it wasn't much. She just said that her grandfather had been alarmed and upset when she told him she had met me. I couldn't understand it all and I was really worried. Then when I got home I had a row with my mother, because I have a friend who is coloured, and she hates coloured people. Then she told me that my father did, too. I was stunned!"

"Go on, Thomas."

"Well, as you know, when I got back to Oxford, I met Sally, and she told me about the Kendals – this was another shock. I was so pleased to meet you all, but when I met Amy I could see she was scared of me...and I was more worried than ever. I was sure that she, like Andrew Shaw, knew something about my father that I didn't. I got more and more curious about him."

Joel was frowning, and slowly rubbing a hand across his chin – his anxious eyes watching Thomas's face. Thomas continued.

"Then something else happened – I came in late the night I stayed at Jade Cottage, and I tripped over at the bottom of the stairs, and I found the safe hidden under the carpet. I was more and more convinced that Amy held the secret of my father's past."

Joel was beginning to feel uneasy. His heart began to thump slowly and menacingly in his chest.

"Joel, you know the Sunday that Amy went in to hospital, and you asked me to search for her keys?"

"You opened the safe and found the box?" asked Joel, softly.

"Yes, Joel. I really am sorry. I know I shouldn't have – but I was overcome with curiosity."

"You must have been very shocked."

"I was devastated."

"Have you told anyone?"

"Only Sally as she was with me. But anyone else? No fear!"

"Just keep it that way, Thomas."

"I will. I'd never tell a living soul, you have my word."

"Thank you, Thomas."

"Joel, I've discovered something else about my father that's even worse."

"Worse?"

"Yes, I'm afraid so..." stammered Thomas.

"What is it?" asked Joel, kindly.

"When I met Fliss she told me that if she ever discovered anything about my father, she would let me know." Thomas told Joel about the letter and the second tape.

"So this Fliss never played it?"

"No, thank goodness!" Thomas took the recorder out of his brief–case, plugged it into the wall, and put in the tape.

"The two people talking are my parents," stated Thomas, flatly, as he pressed the play button.

Thomas and Joel sat in silence as they listened to the tape. Joel's eyebrows raising in disbelief. When the tape finished, Joel ran his hands through his hair.

"Good God!" he exclaimed. "It's unbelievable – I'm truly sorry, Thomas, that you have had to learn all this. It must be dreadful for you."

"Yes, it is, it's been awful. It's made me feel quite ill. I'm also certain that the Special Branch had my father assassinated, and I'm glad. He deserved to die."

"Don't be hard on yourself, Thomas. You are nothing like your father, I know."

"But you never met him, did you?"

"No, but the bits and pieces I've picked up from Amy and Henry gave me a good idea what he was like."

"Do you think we should tell Amy the truth about my father?" Joel was thoughtful.

"Not yet. I think she may have a slight suspicion that your father may have been doing something wrong – but I don't know how she would feel if she knew the truth."

"Yes, I do understand, but I have discovered something else that I do want her to know."

"You mean there's more?" asked Joel, amazed.

"Yes." Thomas went on to tell Joel of Emma's secret. Joel listened in astonishment.

"So Emma and Henry are cousins? That's incredible. Do you have the documents with you?"

"Yes. I've photocopied them for Amy to keep. When we opened Amy's box Sally copied out the family tree that Amy had done. We've written out a new one for her." He handed the documents to Joel, who sat and read through them carefully.

"This is truly amazing – I'm sure Amy will be very excited."

"You are going to tell her?"

"Yes."

Do you think she will be angry when she knows I found her box?"

"No, I think she will be relieved that you know. I will tell her this afternoon after we get to Bishops Fell."

"Thanks, Joel."

“Now, Thomas, there is a lot you won’t know about the past, but I’ll have a word with Amy, and if she agrees, we’ll tell you everything. I can trust you to keep it a secret.”

Thomas stood up and shook Joel’s hand.

“Joel, thank you. It’s been a great relief to talk to you.”

“I’m glad you have, Thomas. It’s been a great strain for Amy all these years – I think it will do her good to talk about it – you are her nephew after all, and her family is your family.”

Thomas returned to Oxford feeling as if a great weight had been lifted from his shoulders.

After his departure, Joel sat at his desk, going over all the facts that Thomas had given him. Joel felt sorry for Thomas. He was such a kind, thoughtful young man, he didn’t deserve this terrible news about his parents.

Joel would have been even more shocked if he had known the truth of what Joanna Kendal had done to Sally.

Joel left the bank at 12 o’clock and went home to change, then drove Amy down to Bishops Fell. They decided to have a lazy day, and on the Sunday morning, if the weather stayed fine, they would tidy up the garden, and then go to the Kings Head for lunch.

Once they had settled into the cottage and had a light lunch, Joel decided to tell Amy about Thomas’s visit. He took her hand and looked into her lovely blue eyes.

“I had a visit from Thomas this morning.”

“Thomas?”

“Yes. Now Amy, I’ve got something to tell you – and I don’t want you to say anything until I have finished.” Amy nodded and looked anxiously at her husband. A hand went up to her hair, and she began twisting strands of it round her fingers.

Joel told Amy all about Thomas’s visit, omitting the tape. She sat fascinated as the story unfolded.

“Poor Thomas!” whispered Amy. “He’s so sweet. He must be devastated.”

“He is, Amy. He’s also sorry he opened your box – but curiosity got the better of him!”

“Of course I forgive him. I was just as curious. Isn’t it amazing about Emma!”

Joel gave Amy the documents from Thomas.

“So my Gran had two other sisters. Even Mr. Brown didn’t mention them. I wondered who the Anna and Amelia were in those letters – and look at my family tree now – look how it’s grown!” And look at all these people in this wedding photo! They could all be my Gran’s relations – isn’t it exciting!

Amy babbled on happily.

“Amy, would you like to talk to Thomas? I think we should tell him everything, don’t you?”

“Oh, yes. It would be such a relief!”

“Shall we invite him down to the Barn next weekend?”

“Oh, yes, that would be great. Let’s ring him now!”

The following Saturday afternoon Thomas and Sally arrived at Brent’s Barn. The weather was still quite warm for March, and the sun shone down on Amy’s beautiful garden, which was full of colour. They were taken up to their rooms to leave their luggage, and then led into the lounge, where they sat in comfort looking out of the patio doors at the garden. Mary, the cook–housekeeper, came in with a tray of home–made biscuits and a pot of tea, which Amy handed round.

Joel looked across at Thomas and Amy, and said, quietly, “We’ll have our talk later, after dinner, when Mary has gone.”

“These biscuits are gorgeous, Amy,” exclaimed Sally. “Where did you find such a cook!”

“We’ve been very lucky. Some time ago we advertised for a husband and wife to be our gardener–cum–handyman and cook–housekeeper. Well, Jack Oliver and his wife Mary applied. When I interviewed them, Jack told me that he used to work for my brother as plumber and handyman. He said that when his wife and daughter died, my brother was very kind to him, and Jack owed him his sanity. Anyway, after Thomas was killed, Jack joined some club in London for bereaved parents, and he met Mary. They later married and moved down here. I’m glad they did. They are a marvellous couple.” Thomas looked across at his aunt.

“It’s nice to know that my father could be so kind.”

"Yes, it is. Jack worshipped him. He was very upset when Thomas died, and is always saying how proud he is to be working for Thomas Kendal's sister."

"He's due to retire in a few years time. He wants to move to the coast to be near to his sister. I don't know what we'll do without them," added Joel.

Mary was a little Irishwoman with sparkling blue eyes, and curly grey hair, which, in her youth, had been jet black. She loved working for the Brents, and was always glad when they entertained. She had laid the table in the dining room beautifully, making sure all the glasses and cutlery were sparkling.

She cooked a superb three-course meal for them all. Starting with battered prawns with a garlic dip, followed by lemon chicken with potatoes and vegetables. After serving the sweet, a raspberry pavlova, and coffee, Mary went home, where Jack would take her for a game of bingo and a few drinks down the local pub.

After dinner Amy and Sally cleared the table and Amy went up to her bedroom to fetch the 'box', which she had brought from the cottage, out of the large safe that was concealed in a wall cupboard. She came back to the table, which was now clear apart from bottles of wine, a bottle of brandy and numerous glasses.

The four of them pulled up their chairs, so that they could talk quietly together. The open fire cast a warm glow over them, and flickering shadows danced over the walls. Joel and Thomas lit cigars and Amy a cigarette. An extractor fan discreetly sucked away the smoke. The curtains were drawn – the doors shut.

"Has Mary gone?" asked Joel.

"Yes," replied Amy. They all looked at one another. Joel spoke first.

"Amy, I think you had better start from the beginning, and tell Thomas and Sally everything that happened after your Gran died."

They all sat in silence as Amy told her story – the story that Thomas and Sally had heard on the tape. When she had finished she was inundated with questions from them.

"Amy," asked Sally. "What happened to that Charles Brown?"

"Oh, Charles Brown! What a nightmare he was following me around and bugging my car, and then in the end, he became a dear friend. He would come and visit me and tell me tales about Gran and Lilli – he never knew the other two. He used to tell me stories about Berlin and the life there. He died a couple of years ago. It was so sad," she added softly.

"What did you think of Fransiska?"

"She was lovely." Amy closed her eyes and shook her head. "When we got back from our honeymoon and found that she had turned up, I nearly died! I thought she would give the whole game away – but fortunately she thought their father died after Dad was born – so she never knew the truth. I would love to have told her about the photo that my Gran kept of her – but I didn't dare, and I knew that my Gran must have adored her and missed her."

"It's a shame she didn't have any children," added Sally.

"I know," replied Amy, "and neither did Lilli, and I couldn't have any in the end. I wonder if it was hereditary?" Thomas put a hand over his aunt's.

"I won't produce any children, now that I know the truth. I don't want to produce another Hitler either."

"Thank you, Thomas." Amy's eyes shimmered with tears.

They talked for a long time, when Thomas looked at Amy and frowned.

"Aunt Amy, why do you think Caroline Kendal came over here? Do you think she was a spy?"

"Oh!" gasped Amy. "We think we have worked it out – you tell them, Joel." Joel lit another cigar and began his tale.

"One day Amy and I were sitting in the Kings Head in Bishops Fell. In the bar was an old farmer, Jerome Smith, the grandfather of Victor who you go riding with, Thomas. Well, Jerome had this story that everyone laughed at."

"What was it?" asked Thomas wide-eyed.

"His story was that during the war he used to hear a plane flying low over his farm, and one day he found a parachute half-buried in one of his fields. He insisted that the Germans were dropping agents – but no one would believe him."

Thomas and Sally looked at each other.

"Amy and I thought he could be right – so we decided to do some investigating. We went to the local archives and searched the church registers and some old newspapers, and we discovered that in the January of 1943 there was a terrible snowstorm, and there was a horrific train crash at Cropwell Junction. 200 people were killed, most of them from this area. There were people of all ages – old, middle–aged, young people, and children.

We think that as a result of these deaths Amy's Gran was sent to Bishops Fell, with Henry as cover. The Germans were sending over agents and dropping them in Jerome's fields. They would make their way to the school where Caroline and the Headmaster, also named Smith, would hide them and give them forged documents using the birth certificates of those people who were killed in the train crash."

"Of course!" cried Thomas. "If the agents were stopped they would have a genuine birth certificate – no–one would check deaths."

"Exactly!" replied Joel. "Then we believe these agents moved freely around England, well away from here."

"The schoolteacher, Mr. Smith, must have contacted Berlin after the train crash, knowing they could make good use of all those people's deaths," exclaimed Sally.

"I'm sure of it," answered Joel.

"Did you do anything about that list of contacts?" asked Thomas. Joel took the list out of the box.

"We don't know about the London ones, but Harold Steele's family had lived in Cropwell for generations, so he must have been a traitor or sympathiser. I don't know what Special Branch said to his son, but he sold Cropwell Manor and went to live abroad not long after your father's death. We also found that Gerald Smith, the Headmaster, had taught Harold Steel's children when they were young, and he was at same university at the same time as the solicitor, James Harrison, so they were all connected. They must all have been traitors."

Thomas and Sally were enthralled. She spoke to Joel.

"It looks like there was a whole bunch of traitors in one place. It would have been the ideal place to drop agents."

"I agree." Thomas looked at his aunt.

"So Caroline Kendal was a German spy – I'm sorry Aunt Amy."

"So am I, Thomas. I adored my grandmother – we were very close – I still find it hard to believe that she kept so much a secret from me. I was very hurt."

"Are we going to tell Grandfather Henry that he is the cousin of Grandmother Emma?" asked Thomas

"I'd love to, Thomas, but it might be a bit risky."

"Couldn't you pretend you've just found some of these documents and photos, as long as Grandfather doesn't see his own birth certificate, or his 'father's' death certificate or the newspaper cuttings, it might be OK."

"I'm not happy about it, Thomas. Henry is far too astute, he might be suspicious," added Joel

"It is a shame, he would be so pleased."

"I feel we should think it over very carefully, first."

"OK, Joel."

The four of them talked late into the night.

Everyone slept late the following morning, then got up and had a cooked breakfast in the large kitchen. The table looked out over the garden, which was bathed in spring sunshine.

After breakfast Amy spoke to Thomas.

"Thomas, I'd like to talk to you in private. Let's walk down to the summerhouse."

The two of them wandered through Amy's lovely garden, and went and sat in the summerhouse together. Amy looked across at her nephew.

"Thomas, I want to talk to you about the future. As Joel and I have no children we are going to leave everything between you and Joel's nieces and nephews. Our money will be shared equally, but I want you to have Jade Cottage." Thomas smiled.

"Thank you, Aunt Amy, that's very kind of you." Amy hesitated for a moment, a hand twisting her hair.

"Thomas, there is something I want you to do for me."

"Of course."

"It's about the contents of the box."

"What do you want me to do with them?"

"Well...I know our family history is rather...shocking...but we can't hide the fact that we descend from Adolf Hitler...and we are a part of history that no–one knows about. I would like you to arrange, that after your death, which will hopefully be after ours, for all the contents of the box to be sent to a museum or the Public Record Office where the history books can be amended. Our family will all be gone by then, so it won't matter. Will you do that for me?"

"I'll do better than that. I will write a book about our family starting from the Second World War. I can arrange for it to be published after my death, and the money can go to a charity."

"That's a wonderful idea, Thomas, thank you." Amy looked up at Thomas, her blue eyes sad. "I do wish you were my son, Thomas. Joel and I have grown to love you very much." Thomas's eyes softened.

"And I wish you and Joel were my parents." Thomas took Amy into his arms and gave her a big hug.

Whilst they had been talking the sun had slipped behind heavy black clouds, which had sneaked up over the horizon. It started to rain.

"Come on, Mum!" laughed Thomas. "Let's get back to the house." He took Amy's hand, and the two of them ran, laughing, through the rain all the way back to the house.

Thomas and Sally stayed until the afternoon. Mary had cooked them all a Sunday lunch, and they had sat afterwards looking out onto the garden, where the flowers and lawns were glistening in the falling rain.

As Thomas and Sally were leaving they met Jack Oliver, who approached Thomas shyly. Jack was a wiry little Cockney, with short silvery hair and grey eyes.

"You're Mr. Kendal's son, then?"

"Yes, I am," smiled Thomas.

"Gor blimey! I knew your old man – he was a great bloke. You must be very proud of 'im."

"Yes, I am. Thank you."

"I never knew you'd been born. It's a real surprise."

"I was born in the Lake District."

"'Course. Your old lady come from there, didn't she?"

"Yes."

"Well, it's nice to 'ave met you, Mr. K."

"Thank you, Jack."

Thomas said farewell to Jack and Mary with mixed feelings.

Thomas and Sally gave Amy and Joel a big hug and a kiss before they left, then set off for Oxford. For a few minutes the sun crept out of the clouds and shone down on them through the rain.

They looked at each other and smiled.

Amy and Joel and Thomas and Sally grew very close, their shared secrets of the past binding them together.

When Thomas finished at Oxford he went on to Warwick University to qualify as a teacher. Sally stayed on at Oxford to finish her last year, and got a job teaching languages at Cropwell Manor Private School, who were prepared to take her without a teaching degree. Thomas got a job at Cropwell Grammar School, eventually teaching disabled children. Like his grandfather, Henry, he was an excellent teacher, and was loved by all his pupils.

Thomas and Sally eventually married. They had a quiet wedding in Cropwell and bought a beautiful thatched cottage on the outskirts of Cropwell. Thomas had a vasectomy to ensure they didn't have children.

Thomas took great care of Henry and Penny, and made them both very happy in their old age.

Thomas and Sally settled down to a happy life together.

They were totally unaware of the existence of Thomas's little daughter – Jade Shaw.

EPILOGUE

Henry and Penny both lived to a good age, their last years being their happiest with the love and care of their adored grandson.

Joanna remained in Spain. She drank heavily and died at the age of 70, lonely and unloved. Her will had never been changed, so everything was left to Thomas.

Thomas and Sally led a happy life together. They kept in touch with Gus and Kal, who both married and had families. They all met up together at least once a year, taking it in turns to visit each other at their respective homes. They all remained lifelong friends.

When Marcus and Emma finally passed away, Thomas inherited Westlake Manor. He and Sally moved up there and turned the manor into a school for disabled children. Renovations were made – a lift was installed and ramps put in for wheelchairs. Some of the beautiful bedrooms were turned into small dormitories for children who would be resident during the school terms. A swimming pool was put in and the stables were extended for small ponies for the children to ride. Thomas and Sally taught the children, and employed part–time teachers to help and take over when Thomas and Sally needed time off. A doctor or nurse was always in residence twenty-four hours a day.

Amy and Joel made regular visits to Westlake Manor, and spent much time with the children. After the death of her parents, Amy took her precious photos out of the 'box' and had them framed and hung on the walls of her cottage in Bishops Fell.

After the death of her husband Amy spent a lot of time with Thomas and Sally. She eventually died at Bishops Fell – like her grandmother. Thomas was heartbroken.

Thomas had a good life at Westlake Manor, putting right his father's wrongs. He was loved by his wife and all the children he cared for, and they loved him in return. If anyone deserved the title of 'Saint Thomas' it was Thomas Kendal junior.

During the first few years at Westlake Manor Thomas received another shock which rocked his life. It was in the March after his fortieth birthday. He and Sally were sitting having breakfast. Sally was gazing out of the window at the spring sunshine creeping through the trees, and Thomas was reading the newspaper. All was quiet until Sally heard Thomas gasp.

"Thomas, what's wrong?" she asked in alarm. He looked pale and shocked. He tapped the paper with his hand.

"This...this article," he stammered. Frowning, Sally got up, walked round the table, and leaned over his shoulder, her soft brown hair tickling his cheek.

"It was the name Jade that caught my eye – because of Jade Cottage."

Sally read the article. It was about a young girl called Jade Shaw. She had been out celebrating her twentieth birthday when the car she was in was involved in an accident. It said that she was the daughter of Felicity Shaw, who now owned Shaw's Travel Agency, after the death of her father. Jade was now in the new Accident Hospital in Barnet in Hertfordshire, on a life-support system.

"I think she's my daughter," said Thomas in a strangled whisper, his hands shaking.

"Your daughter. Oh Thomas!" cried Sally. "Are you sure?"

"She must be. It says here it was her twentieth birthday."

"I didn't realise you were that friendly," replied Sally, her heart sinking.

"We weren't, but we spent her last evening together at Oxford, and I had bought her a little present...we went back to my flat...we were both a bit drunk...and she stayed the night...it wasn't planned...it just happened."

Sally took a deep breath to help her recover from the shock. She gripped Thomas's shoulder, her voice husky with emotion.

"Do you want to go and see her – before it's too late?" Thomas gripped her hand.

"Could we?"

"Why not?"

Thomas and Sally quickly made arrangements for the children, and half an hour later were speeding south in their chauffeur-driven car. Thomas's handsome face looked pale and gaunt. Sally held her husband's hand tightly. He was shocked and trembling.

After a silent journey, their chauffeur dropped them off outside the hospital, and went off to get himself a bite to eat and a pot of tea. His mobile phone tucked in his pocket.

Holding hands Thomas and Sally walked through the main doors of the hospital into a large reception area. Standing at the desk was a tall, smartly dressed woman, with short red hair. She turned at their approach, and gasped.

"Thomas Kendal. What on earth are you doing here?"

"I think you know why, Fliss," said Thomas quietly.

"Let's go where we can talk," she replied softly.

They moved away to the corner of the reception area, out of earshot of other people. Thomas introduced Sally and Fliss.

"Jade, she is my daughter, isn't she?"

"Yes, but how did you find out?"

"It was in the paper."

"Of course."

"Well?"

"Yes, Thomas, she is."

"Why didn't you tell me?"

"There didn't seem any point, Thomas. We hardly knew each other, and we had separate lives."

"How bad is she?"

"Very poorly, I'm afraid. She has a collapsed lung, a ruptured spleen and other internal injuries." Thomas took a deep breath.

"I'm so sorry, Fliss. May...may we see her?"

"Of course."

The three of them walked slowly towards the lift. Whilst they were waiting Thomas spoke to Fliss.

"Did you never marry, Fliss?"

"No, but I do have someone. We have never married, because Jade hates him."

"Hates him! But why?"

"Because he's crippled." Thomas and Sally looked at each other in silent dismay.

"What happened, Fliss?" asked Sally, kindly.

"He was a soldier – he lost half a leg in an explosion. Jade says it makes her feel ill to see him limping about."

Thomas and Sally were horrified. They looked at each other again without speaking, as the lift arrived. As they got into the lift Fliss looked up at Thomas.

"I've read what you have done with Westlake Manor. I think it's wonderful of you both."

"Thank you, Fliss."

"It's a good job Jade doesn't know you are her father."

"Why?"

"She would probably have gone up to Westlake Manor and blown it up!"

"She...she's...been difficult, then?" stammered Thomas, as they got out of the lift.

"I'm afraid so," replied Fliss, sadly.

They walked along a corridor, when Fliss spoke to Thomas again.

"By the way, were those tapes any use to you?" Thomas felt sick. "Er...yes...they told me what I wanted to know."

"Was it bad?"

"Er...it wasn't good."

"I'm sorry." They stopped suddenly outside a door. "She's in here."

Thomas's heart was pounding as the door was opened, and he saw his daughter for the first time. She lay pale and still, her eyes closed, her red hair, just like her mother's, spread motionless over the pillow. A monitor beside the bed was bleeping slowly. Her body was full of tubes – one up her nose, one in her neck and another in her hand. Others were covered by the sheet.

Thomas walked up to the bed with Sally and Fliss behind him. He looked down at his daughter – she was so beautiful – her skin was freckled, like her mother's, her nose and mouth were like Emma's. He stared at her for a long time – his heart gripped in an icy hand. Tears of dismay, shock and love filled his blue eyes.

"I don't want her to die," whispered Fliss in a choked voice. Thomas turned to face her.

"Turn it off, Fliss."

"What!"

"The life-support, Fliss – have it turned off."

"But why?"

There was an uncomfortable silence.

Sally touched Thomas's arm.

"Tell her, Thomas. She has a right to know. Fliss has kept you a secret for twenty years. I'm sure we can trust her."

Thomas looked at Fliss, and put his hands on her shoulders. He looked down into her puzzled green eyes.

"I've learnt the truth about my father, Fliss. He.... he was the grandson of Adolf Hitler."

Fliss turned white, her eyes widened in horror.

"Thomas, you can't be serious!" she choked.

"I'm afraid it's true, Fliss, and my father was just as bad."

"And Jade is the same!" cried Fliss. "Oh, God, she's always hated anyone who wasn't perfect – I should have guessed..."

"No, Fliss, there are lot of people in the world like that, believe me."

"Do you have evidence?"

"Yes, I do. That is why Sally and I have not had any children."

"So there's no mistake?"

"No."

Fliss sank onto the chair beside the bed, covered her face with slender hands, and wept.

Thomas and Sally stayed for some time with Fliss. They sat and talked together in shocked, quiet voices. When they finally left,

Thomas leaned over his dying daughter and gently kissed her cheek, his heart full of anguish.

Fliss walked with Thomas and Sally to the main doors of the hospital. Sally rang for their chauffeur to collect them, then the three of them kissed goodbye.

"Keep in touch with us, Fliss," begged Sally.

"I will. I promise."

Fliss waved to them as they drove away. Thomas was silent all the way home. He gripped Sally's hand tightly, and her heart went out to her beloved, tormented husband. When they got home, Thomas went up to their room...and wept.

Jade Shaw died the following day. The last of Hitler's descendants was gone forever.

The funeral took place the following week. On top of Jade's coffin was a heart–shaped spray of red roses. The card attached to it read, simply – "Thomas and Sally."

Thomas spent the rest of his life compiling his book of his amazing family history, fulfilling his promise to Amy. He dedicated his book to her memory.

After his death the documents from Amy's box were sent to the Publice Record Office at Kew, and the coins to the British Museum.

Thomas's book was an instant success, and the proceeds were used for the upkeep of Westlake Manor which was kept on by trustees as a school for disabled children.

Thomas's book was called – 'SLEEPING DOGS'

END OF THE LINE

ADOLF HITLER = Christine Koner

(Caroline Kendal)

1889-1945 | 1917-1990

HEINRICH KONER = Penelope Hall

(Henry Kendal)

1942-2022 | 1942-2024

THOMAS KENDAL snr.=Joanna Westlake   AMY KENDAL

1962-1991   1963-2033   1967-2050

THOMAS KENDAL jnr. = Felicity Shaw

1991-2077

JADE SHAW

2012-2032

USEFUL ADDRESSES

The Family Record Centre

1 Myddleton Street

London EC1R 1UW

(Registers of births, deaths, and marriages, deaths overseas, adoptions, and census returns)

The Public Record Office

Ruskin Avenue

Kew

Surry TW9 4DU

(Historic documents, army navy, merchant navy, and RAF records, etc.)

The Anglo-German Family History Society

Mrs Jenny Towey

20 Skylark Rise

Woolwell

Plymouth

Devon PL6 7SN

The Leicestershire Family History Society

Membership Secretary (2001)

Mr Tom Shaw

33 Sussex Road

South Wigston

Leicester LE18 4WP

Coming soon from the pen of Norma Rawlings

DANGEROUS SONG

Claudia Morris marries an Italian singer, Atillio Rossini, and goes to live with him in Italy. Claudia's happiness is short-lived when she discovers just how much Atillio's family hates her. Things are not helped by her firm belief that the family has connections with the mafia!

Eventually, Claudia has twin boys, but her fear of the family and a new pregnancy, cause her to flee. With the help of her sister she escapes to England - where she has her daughter - Lucy.

As the years pass, Claudia's husband and sons become world famous singers, but then, to her horror, Lucy also wants to be singer. Terrified that Lucy will discover the secret of her father's family, Claudia tries desperately to hide the truth that will lead them all into danger.